GILM!
EVERYBODY'S SAYING IT!

BRIAN CORLEY

ISBN (e-book edition): 979-8-9892708-0-4
ISBN (Paperback edition): 979-8-9892708-1-1
Library of Congress Control Number: 2023920037

Cover design by Ellen Lampl
Interior design by Jessica Reed

Printed and bound in the USA
First printing 2024

Published by Electric Fern in 2024
www.brian-corley.com

For The Mars McClanes

Mic Check,
Is This Thing On?

Finding your niche as a new kid in high school is a balancing act. Like standing tiptoe on the top rung of a stepladder while stretching toward a shelf almost out of reach. This may sound oddly specific, but it was exactly what Geoff Smith was doing on the sales floor of his dad's store, Curio City.

Geoff had rolled his eyes when his dad told him the idea for the name. His dad loved puns, which was a very dad thing to love, but he was also obsessed with the arcane and mystical, which was not, traditionally, a very dad thing to love at all.

The store was a converted Victorian house nestled in the trendy Belmont District in Southeast Portland. The exterior was similar to those of the other old houses on the street, but instead of a multicolored painted-lady style, Curio City stood in various shades of grey and black.

Towering bookshelves contained histories of elves and fairies, biographies of magicians and wizards, recipe books for spells, and blah blah blah, you get it. Geoff didn't really care. All he knew was that the business made his dad happy and, surprisingly, enough money to uproot them both to a new city.

The rooms on the second floor, accessible by a hand-carved staircase, were full of vintage taxidermy, suits of armor here and there, and plants you wouldn't normally find in a nursery (think mandrake and other nightshades instead of roses and ferns).

But back to Geoff and his precarious position.

He'd been stuck with one hand against the wall and one leg in the air, trying to maintain his balance. He figured that if he pushed off just right, he could grab the miniature skeleton's case off the top shelf with one hand, push himself backward with the other, and then land where he started, with both feet firmly on the top rung of the stepladder.

Of course, there was a taller ladder in the basement that would eliminate the need for this type of acrobatics, but then he'd have to put the stepladder away upstairs and haul the other one up, so no.

He just needed to use his leverage to inch himself a little bit higher . . .

"Ow!"

He'd inadvertently found the business end of another loose staple by jamming his finger into it right as he was about to push off for his very well-thought-out stunt. The old house was full of quirks and poorly patched fixes, and Geoff had shown a unique aptitude for uncovering them.

"You OK?" his dad called from another room.

Geoff stepped down the ladder and sucked at the blood that was sure to come from the nick. "I almost had it."

"Are you bleeding?"

"I don't know, maybe."

His dad appeared at his side and winced in sympathetic pain. He pulled a silk paisley handkerchief from his jacket and offered it up like an old-timey professor. Which he was. He'd just taken a professorship at Reese University. Partly to maintain his credibility as an expert in the occult and paranormal, but the health insurance was pretty good too.

"Dad, thank you, but what do you want me to do with that handkerchief? I'll be fine." Geoff slid the stepladder over a few inches and surveyed the distance between it and the glass half-dome display that held a tiny skeleton with gnarly clawed hands that dwarfed the rest of its body. It was probably just old monkey bones that someone tinkered with to make a quick buck. Whatever; his dad had crazy things like that all over the store, and someone had just bought this one online.

Geoff stepped back up on the ladder and stretched out his hand.

"Wait! Do not give it blood," his dad said with a note of panic, in stark contrast to his normal professorial voice, rich and worn with use.

Geoff laughed. "I can just wipe off the glass if I get blood on it. It's no big deal."

His dad ran a hand through his salt-and-pepper hair. "Hey, why don't you come down and wash your finger in the sink in the back? I think I can reach the piece a little easier."

"I almost have it, it's right here."

"Geoff, please just come down."

His dad was a weird guy. Mostly good-weird, but sometimes just weird-weird. Like when he was all "Don't touch that with your eyes open!" or "Hold your breath when you look at that!" And now, "Don't give it blood!"

OK, Mr. Unwritten-rules-the-rest-of-the-world-should-already-know. Guess I'll just go back to wondering why we moved here and left everyone we've ever known back in Texas.

His dad sighed. "I shouldn't bring pieces like this to the store. They're too dangerous and only meant for certain clients, anyway. I'll take it back to the house for safekeeping."

"Safekeeping? I thought we were shipping it."

"That's right. Still, there are some things that shouldn't be here." His dad rubbed his eyes. "So, how are things at school?"

Classic redirect.

"Tremendous. Couldn't be better. I wish we didn't have weekends so I could be there right now."

"Hey, what did I tell you about wishes?"

Oh my god. So many rules.

"Always wish for something great," they said in unison.

"Good, remember that. So, I take it you haven't found your groove yet?"

But Geoff just stared at the floor. He wasn't interested in responding to a question his dad already knew the answer to.

A sympathetic dimple quirked his dad's cheek. "Don't worry, son. Just be yourself. Do you remember how you made friends back in Houston?"

"Yeah, Dad. I was five. It's easy to make friends when you're five. You're just like, *Hey, can you believe we're five?* And then the other kids are like, *Yeah, being five is great! Now let's run feral around the class-room and be best friends for the next ten years or so.*"

"Well, have you tried running around a room and making a bunch of noise with your classmates?"

"Not yet, Dad. Maybe I'll try that tomorrow."

A throat was cleared a few feet away and mercifully brought an end to the conversation.

"How much is this?" asked a kid about Geoff's age. He was dressed all in black, which included his dyed hair underneath a top hat. And a cape. Yes, the kid was wearing a top hat and cape. Geoff's dad wasn't a goth per se, but he wasn't exactly *not* a goth either. The goths loved his store, and he had quickly become their new king.

"Oh, hi, Kyle," Geoff's dad said. "That taxidermied bat is rumored to have belonged to Jimmy Page from Led Zeppelin."

Kyle stared for a moment. "Led Zeppelin. Is that like an old TV show?"

"My boy," Geoff's dad said. He said things like that when he was slightly annoyed with someone but still wanted to be nice. "They're a band. A wonderful band. You are going to love discovering them. Now, this is your basic guardian ward." Geoff's dad started gesticulating like an actor on a Broadway stage. "Its mere presence is a signal to the mid and lesser malevolent spirits to find somewhere else to spend their time."

"But what if I want to be visited by darker spirits?" Kyle asked.

Geoff's dad's forehead scrunched. "We've talked about this, Kyle."

"OK, so, how much?" Kyle asked.

"What does the price tag say?"

"Can you do like fifty less?"

"For you, that works. Right this way." Geoff's Dad led Kyle to the store's bronze and copper antique cash register. He disappeared below the counter, only to return with an enormous ledger, which he plopped down with a satisfying thump.

His dad always made a big show of a sale. He unscrewed a fountain pen with a flourish. "Ah, the written word. No magnet can jumble it, and no internet outage can deny its existence," he said as he scribbled down the item number he'd assigned to the bat and described what it looked like and its mystical properties, if any—the usual.

"But what if the paper gets wet?" Kyle asked.

His dad looked up from the ledger.

"Or if there's a fire," Geoff said. "Fire can pretty much destroy anything, right?"

He gave Geoff a side-eye and handed Kyle the pen. "I just need you to sign here."

Kyle leaned down and scratched out his signature.

The professor nodded and shut the book with another satisfying thunk. "I already have your email, so we don't need that. Geoff?"

Geoff produced the store's iPad, and Kyle handed over his card. Paper and pen may have been indelible, but the rest of the world ran on electronic data transfer. After a quick swipe, Geoff returned the card. "Just sign here."

Kyle made a few squiggles with his finger and tipped his top hat. "Pleasure doing business with you, sirs."

"Hey, Kyle. You go to Alder High School, right?" Geoff's dad asked.

"I do. Go 'Varks," Kyle said, holding up two fingers in a V. "'Varks" was short for "Aardvarks," the name of the school's teams, and Geoff couldn't tell if Kyle was being sarcastic or not.

"Yes, go 'Varks," his dad said. "Geoff just started there a few weeks ago. This is my son, Geoff, by the way."

Once again, Kyle tipped his hat.

"Hi," Geoff replied.

"Maybe you two could be friends."

"Maybe you two could be friends"? Really, Dad?

"I don't believe in friendship," Kyle replied. He said it in the same tone as the *Go 'Varks* bit, but this time, Geoff didn't mistake the sentiment. It wasn't uninclusive, necessarily, just uninviting.

"Of course, of course," Geoff's dad said. "Want me to box this up for you?"

By "box," Geoff's dad meant "crate." The man would literally go into the back room and custom-build a wooden crate filled with straw.

"No, thank you," Kyle said.

"But it's raining."

Kyle unfurled his cape and stowed the bat underneath. "See you on Wednesday, Professor Smith."

An antique bell clanged against the door as Kyle exited the shop.

"What's on Wednesday?" Geoff asked.

"I'm not sure, my boy, but I hope it's not a dark omen of things to come."

"Don't 'my boy' me, Dad. I know what that means."

His dad shook his head and grinned. "You want to go home?"

"To Houston? Yes."

"Geoff," his father said, and squeezed his shoulder. "You'll get used to it here, you'll see. You might even like it."

"I doubt it."

His dad sighed. "I know it's a lot of change. Hey, you want takeout?"

His dad wasn't a bad cook. In fact, he was a pretty good one. But he also had a knack for finding amazing restaurant takeout, and if there was one thing Geoff liked about Portland so far, it was the food. "Yeah, let's get Thai."

"OK." His dad slung a satchel around his shoulder and trotted up the stepladder. "I'll just grab this little gremlin and ship it from home."

Geoff rolled his eyes. "A gremlin. Dad, please. A carny stitched alligator hands to a monkey skeleton or something a hundred years ago. That is not the remnant of a supernatural creature."

"If you say so, son," his dad said, and set the "gremlin" down on the counter with both hands.

"Also, if you're so worried about that, why would you want it in the house with us?"

"I'm not worried," his dad said. "I'm concerned, so I'm taking precautions. Why, are you worried?"

"I'm not," Geoff said. "We just have a lot of weird stuff at home. Like that wooden gnome you keep in the office."

"So, you want me to keep the gremlin here tonight?"

That was a big yes from Geoff. Fake or not, that thing gave him the heebie-jeebies. Those teeth were sharp like a monkey's but were more like a bunch of jagged little Vs instead of primate teeth. Normally, the illusion of something like that would fall apart upon closer inspection—you could see the poorly matched joints or cheap glue in the bones—but this specimen looked like it came straight from a university archive or something. It was unsettling, but Geoff wasn't about to let on to his father.

"Whatever gets me Thai food faster," Geoff said instead.

"OK, we can leave it at the store. I'll just need to put it in here overnight." His dad held his hand over a glass display while whispering something under his breath. He unlocked the display and carefully deposited the gremlin inside.

"You're going to keep it safe in a glass case?" Geoff asked.

"This isn't just any glass case," his dad replied. "The sigils inscribed around the edges are designed to hold much higher levels of naughty inside."

"Dad, anyone with a rock or hammer could smack through that in no time. Ohh, you said 'inside,' that's right. Gremlin, I forgot."

As he moved to shut the case, his dad slipped a leather-bound book out and tucked it into his vintage satchel. The professor whispered a few more words under his breath, locked the case back up, and turned to leave.

"What's that?" Geoff asked. To most people, his dad's sleight of hand would have gone unnoticed, but Geoff had fifteen years' experience observing his father's quirks.

"Nothing."

"Dad, I saw you put that book in your bag."

"Like I said, Geoff. Some things are too dangerous to be left unattended at the store."

The Mysterious Sheet Music

Geoff sat up in his bed and ran both hands through his scraggly brown hair. He rubbed his eyes and stared out the rain-dappled window into the darkness. *It's always raining here,* he thought. *I wish it could be sunny and normal for one day . . . wait, no. I wish for two billion dollars.*

His dad was right. He should wish for something great. The professor drummed it into his head after Geoff would throw tantrums, saying things like *I wish we never moved here* or *I wish they still made white chocolate almond ice cream!* Which wasn't a bad wish, but Geoff had decided that wishing for two billion dollars could make something like that happen, and a lot more.

"Geoff," his dad called from the kitchen below. "You're late! I mean, if you're not already dressed, you're going to be late for school."

"Yeah, Dad, I'm dressed," Geoff lied. "Be down in a minute."

Geoff sighed. At least in Houston, the sun would have the common decency to be out at this time of the morning, even where they lived in the suburbs. But the sun was never out in Portland, Oregon. It was pitch-black at seven thirty in the morning, and on top of that, constantly raining.

The sun wasn't all he missed, though. He missed the tight-knit group of friends he'd left behind. They'd just formed a band.

They'd been building toward it for years. Geoff learned how to play the guitar while the guys worked on other things, like understanding social media marketing and procrastinating.

Still, after all that time, one of the guys actually had started up a shared drive, and they'd recorded a couple of songs. None of them were very good, but Geoff was sure they were on the brink of something great.

His dad always said no one was really good at anything when they first started. That you had to be bad at something before you became good, and blah blah blah. Geoff forgot whatever he said after that.

He'd been writing in his spare time, though. It was critical to the persona he was trying on for his new school. He'd been listening to the Dandy Warhols since he was a kid, and they'd started out in Portland, so maybe he could too. He stared around the blank walls of the finished attic that was his bedroom.

In Texas, attics were hot, dusty crawl spaces filled with pink insulation and spiderwebs, but here in the Pacific Northwest, they had walls and everything—everything but central A/C and heat. The attic had two windows, though, so they'd put in a portable unit.

Geoff wondered if his dad had agreed to his idea of converting the space because it gave him the opportunity to have the study he'd always wanted.

"Geoff," his dad called from the kitchen.

"Coming!" Geoff said. He rolled the blanket back and rummaged through his dresser drawers for a suitable graphic tee to wear under a flannel. He rubbed some deodorant under his arms and was ready to go in no time. He grabbed his backpack off a couple of boxes he hadn't unpacked yet and navigated the slight curve down the narrow steps. He gently toed the half-open door wider, careful not to catch his dad in the back of the head again on his entrance into the kitchen.

His dad huddled over the coffeemaker, pouring the remaining contents of the glass carafe into his buffalo plaid travel thermos. The man loved coffee, so much so that Geoff thought it was one of the main reasons they'd moved to Portland, but he wouldn't let Geoff touch the stuff. Said it would stunt his growth or mess with his memory—really whatever was convenient on the day.

"Big day today?" Geoff's dad asked. He asked the same question every morning.

"That's right," Geoff said.

"Need a lift to school?"

"Nah, thanks, though. I can ride my bike."

"You sure? It's pretty slick out there."

"I mean, yeah, you could take me, but then I'd have to walk home, and it will still be just as rainy."

"I could always pick you up after school."

Geoff imagined his father rolling up in his dark grey sprinter van, blasting classical music, and rolling down the window to shout that he loved him in front of the entire school.

"Pass."

His dad chuckled.

Wait. What is that?

Something pulled at Geoff's thoughts. Something he could sense was small but felt like it had its own outsized gravity. He scanned the space before zeroing in on his target. The leather-bound book from the store was resting on the table in the dining room.

His dad had brought home literally thousands of books, so why would that one stand out? It was hard to describe its color, but "blood-red" would be a close approximation. The cover was scarred with all sorts of carvings, and the pages were staggered and ragged rather than cut neatly together. Something within him said he needed to get a closer look. He wanted to feel the book's weight in his hands.

"Don't," Geoff's dad said.

It caught Geoff by surprise. His dad wasn't the jumpy sort and definitely wasn't one to be described as stern, and yet that "don't" had a dark tone to it.

"Sorry," his dad said, striding over to the table and hooking the book into the palm of his hand. "This is a new one, and I haven't had the chance to read it yet."

If it wasn't the least believable excuse Geoff had ever heard, it was in the top three, along with his dad's last-gasp attempts to keep the idea of Santa alive. *You know, time is relative, and Santa doesn't experience it like the rest of us do. Our one night, to him, is thousands, blah blah blah, he is working nonstop to bring presents to the world, blah blah blah.*

It had made young Geoff feel so bad for Santa that one night he spent an hour wailing into his pillow before his dad finally came clean.

So, despite his dad's best efforts, there was more of a chance of the sun making an appearance on a Portland winter morning than of Geoff not reading that book. He had to get to the bottom of why his dad was being so weird about it.

"It's OK," Geoff said. "I was actually looking at the protein bar next to it. I'm hungry."

It was a good lie. Believable, since he hadn't eaten, and Geoff needed to get moving if he was going to make it to school on time. Not that he cared much about punctuality, but a guy named Will hung around at the bike racks and had a really cool hobby of picking on people who didn't grow up in his neighborhood their whole life.

Especially if he caught them out on their own.

The closer it got to the bell, the fewer targets there were for Will, so time was of the essence.

His dad's grip loosened on the book as Geoff grabbed his raincoat from a hook and opened the back door.

"Bye, son—"

"Like the buffalo said to his kid," they vocalized in unison, Geoff more under his breath than his dad.

His dad loved that joke. Bison—bye, son. You get it.

Minor-Key
Meet-and-Greet

"Hey, new kid," Will yelled, even though he was just ten feet away. Geoff ignored him in the hopes that Will was yelling at someone else. "New kid, hey! I'm talking to you."

He wasn't yelling at someone else.

"Hi, Will," Geoff said.

"What kind of bike is that?"

"I don't know . . . a dark green one?" Geoff kept his head down, focused on locking up his bike and avoiding eye contact with Will.

"Oh, ha ha," Will said. "See you and your dark green bike after school."

"Yeah, OK. My name is Geoff, by the way. Good to know someone at this school is looking forward to seeing me."

"I didn't mean it like that," Will said.

Geoff gave his lock a double pull to make sure it was secured and wondered why Will hadn't shoved or punched him yet. Where was his line? Was he a real bully or just a loud talker?

Plunk!

A crumpled can bounced off Geoff's forehead. Its remaining contents spilled down his nose and the front of his rain jacket. Will erupted in laughter.

OK, a real bully, then.

The first bell of the day rang to signal the trek to first period. Geoff trudged across the soggy lawn into the clay-bricked, classical-revival-style public school.

The halls were packed with students who all seemed to know exactly where they were going, unlike certain new kids. Geoff checked for landmarks, like the wall with the musical sign-ups. Wait, wouldn't there be more than one sign-up poster? Of course, there would be more than one, they were marketing.

He searched for more clues, but the blue lockers made all the halls look the same. Was he even in the right wing of the building? That second turn was always tricky. Or was it the third?

The traffic in the hallway thinned, which meant that the last bell was seconds away from separating the on-time from the tardy. The familiar from the lost. Geoff was tired of being late to history. It was embarrassing. He'd been working up the nerve to try to ask Corinne Shelby out for a couple of weeks now, but there was no way she would be interested in some hapless new guy with no sense of direction.

Corinne had dark hair and minty green eyes . . . or were they grey? Hazel maybe? Geoff didn't really know the difference between green and hazel, so he'd decided to call them grazel. Only to himself, so far. He was still workshopping the idea.

Where is the classroom?

The bell rang.

Oh my god, it's right there.

It was as though the classroom door magically appeared as soon as the bell sounded. Like some sort of enchantment had kept it hidden almost every morning until it was too late. Geoff hurried inside.

"Mr. Smith," Mr. Dent said. "You're late."

Mr. Dent was the type of teacher to wear short sleeves and a tie. He had the outline of hair on his head, but he shaved it bald because he preferred to make the decision instead of nature. Geoff gave him a tight smile and walked toward his seat, painfully aware of every step he made along the way.

Just act casual, Geoff. Does this type of walking make me seem confident, like I know where I'm going, or am I walking too fast?

He slumped into his seat.

"Hope everyone did their reading last night. The Salem witch trials were—"

Mr. Dent sighed and crossed his arms as the zipper on Geoff's backpack interrupted his introduction to the day's lesson.

"Mr. Smith, perhaps you could lead the discussion on the Salem witch trials?"

Geoff was only half paying attention while fishing around for a pencil, so he didn't quite catch Dent's tone. More of a *Hey, are you going to teach this class or let me?* rather than a *Hey, I'm curious, can you share some of your knowledge?*

"Sure, I guess," Geoff said. "Did you know that it's a myth that anyone was burned at the stake? Most of them were hanged. The whole stake-burning thing was more of a European tradition."

"That is very dark, Mr. Smith."

"Sorry. My dad is big into stuff like that and is always dropping weird facts. Everything I know about the Salem witch trials is against my will."

"My dad likes witches," some kid scoffed from the back. A low rumble of laughter followed.

"Alright, that's enough," Mr. Dent said. "Mr. Smith may be right. I'm not sure. That was not in the assignment, so I'll need to fact-check that, but today we'll be talking about . . ."

"Nice fun fact," Corrinne whispered. A grazel eye peeked through strands of dark black hair that framed her face.

Geoff tried not to smile too wide. Corrinne Shelby didn't talk to him that often, and he didn't want to scare her off.

"Did you know frogs swallow with their eyes?" Geoff whispered back.

"Gross."

Geoff's chest tightened. Why did he have to say that? He could have just played it cool with his small victory and maybe said something to her after class, but no, he had to keep shooting his mouth off—

"Is that true?"

Geoff grinned, crooked an eyebrow, and watched Corinne's eye squint into a half-moon through strands of dark hair.

* * *

The bell rang, and the class sprang to life as Mr. Dent shouted his final points and reminded them about their reading for the night, but all Geoff could focus on was Corinne. And whether he was standing weird. Or doing something strange with his hands. Was he breathing weird?

"That's cool that you still take handwritten notes for class," Corinne said. "Strange, but cool."

"Yeah, my dad kind of drilled that into me. Something about mastering the magic of pen to page, or that magic can mess with technology. I don't know, he says a lot of things like that."

"That's . . . cool."

Oh my god, what are you saying? Why would you choose to share that information? You already know people think your dad is weird, and those were people who liked you. "Is it?" Geoff said.

"It's something."

"I move to strike the last sentence from the record, Your Honor."

Corinne chuckled as she finished putting her stuff away in a stylish patchwork satchel. "Hey, have you seen the sign-ups for *Wicked?*" Corinne asked.

"Oh, is that the musical they're doing?"

"Yeah."

Geoff slung his backpack around his shoulder and moved toward the door. "I'm not really into musicals." *You idiot, she obviously just asked you about something she likes.*

"Why?"

"I don't know. I feel like you could just say it."

"Instead of singing it?" Corinne replied. She

shrugged. "That would be boring, who wants to go see a show where people just talk to each other?"

"Plenty," Geoff said. "They're called plays."

What are you doing? Why are these words coming out of your mouth? You like her, remember?

"So, you're up here, and I'm down here then?" Corinne asked. She used her hands to illustrate what she'd just said and make Geoff feel like a cocky idiot. Mission accomplished.

You're dead. You are a dead man. "No, it's not like that. I'm sorry. I just—"

"Don't like music?" Corinne said.

"Oh no, I love music. I just use my words for talking. Like, what would you do if I just started singing right now?"

Corinne looked him straight in the eye. "I would love it. No one has ever sung to me before."

OK, wasn't expecting that. Geoff shrugged his backpack higher. "Well, maybe I could change that. I'm in a band." *I'm in a band. Listen to yourself. You just said you're in a band. You said that out loud. Did you think that would sound cool? Because, guess what? It did not.*

The corners of her mouth curled. "You're in a band?"

"Yeah." Geoff tried not to blink. Sure, the rest of his band was back in Texas, and they'd never played a show, but he was already in too deep.

Corinne squinted. "Like covers, or . . ."

"No, I write my own stuff."

"Oh, cool." She nodded. "That's cool."

"Hey, would you like to go out sometime?" Geoff asked.

After weeks spent workshopping the perfect segue or casual invitation, he'd just blurted it out. *God, Geoff, why are you like this?*

"Maybe," she said. "So, you're a songwriter. Can you rhyme a word with 'orange'?"

"'Door hinge.' I know it's two words, but they have the same syllable count."

Geoff had seen Eminem use that example in a video once, so he had that one chambered and ready to go. It wasn't the first time someone had issued that particular challenge.

"Wow, I'm impressed," she said.

They walked shoulder to shoulder in the hall, their steps finding the same beat like they were synced to a metronome. Just them against the flow of bodies hurrying in every direction as they made their way to their classes. Or to musical sign-up sheets like the one coming up on the right.

"Tell you what," Corinne said. "If you write me a song that rhymes something with the word 'film,' I'll take you for pizza."

Wait, is she asking me out? Is pizza a good date food? Do I want to have grease on my fingers all night? I guess I could use a knife and fork, but who does that? Geoff, pull yourself together. It's pizza. You love pizza, and you've already criticized her choices. Just say yes, but be cool about it.

"Alright," Geoff said. *That was pretty good.*

"And it has to be a word that people use. No dead languages."

Geoff chuckled. *She knows how to make a deal.* "You're on."

"You know, Geoff, there is a fine line between confidence and cockiness."

Oh no. Was that cocky? I just laughed because I'm excited. "I didn't—" Geoff started to say.

"Have it to me by midnight."

"Wow, OK." Geoff scratched the back of his head. "I guess it's like Albert Einstein said, 'I don't need time, I need a deadline.'"

Corinne's eyes narrowed. "Duke Ellington said that, Geoff."

"That's right," Geoff said. "The Duke."

"That's John Wayne."

"What?"

"John Wayne is the Duke; Duke Ellington is just Duke."

"Wow," Geoff said. "You know a lot of things. Hey, um . . . think I could get your number?"

A dimple creased her cheek as she looked him up and down. "Give me your phone."

Geoff's hand shot to his pocket before he could realize how desperate he might look by moving so fast. Whatever, he thought. If Corinne wanted to put her number in his phone, he wasn't going to stop her.

He unlocked it, brought up a blank contact, and handed it over.

It would be funny if she just ran away right now. I mean, not funny for me, but objectively funny.

Corinne passed his phone back.

Nice, she put a black heart after her name. Wait, is that good or bad? Heart is good, but is black heart good? Does it really matter? Just go with it.

"Rhyme 'film,' real word." Her finger pointed to emphasize each word. "By midnight."

This will be easy. Now, what rhymes with "film"? Wait, this should be easy. His stomach dropped. *This is not easy.*

"Is this because I said I don't like musicals?" Geoff asked above the din of the hallway.

"It is one hundred percent because you said you don't like musicals. I've been in theater since elementary school and was obviously inviting you to join."

"Why don't I just sign up then?" Geoff pivoted to the sign-up sheet.

"Oh no, it's too late for that. We only want the committed."

Corinne was being kind of flirty, but she definitely wanted to inflict some pain.

"Yeah, alright, I'll have something for you tonight. Excited for some free pizza," Geoff said.

"We'll see," Corinne said before fading into the flow of students to head to her next class.

"Stilm"? No, not a word. "Hilm"—nope. "Pilm" . . . oh my god, nothing rhymes with "film."

The Haunting Melody

Geoff slammed the back door of the house and unzipped his raincoat.

He kicked off his rain-soaked sneakers and tugged at his waterlogged socks, slapping them with a satisfying thwack against the black hexagonal tiles of the kitchen floor. Geoff had had to walk his bike home after finding both tires flat after school. No doubt thanks to all Will's free time during school hours.

He grabbed an apple from the fruit bowl on the kitchen counter and padded his way to the dining room. The dryness of the old wooden floor soothed his wet bare feet. He drummed his fingers along the top of the table. He'd been trying to hum a tune for his new song, but so far, nothing had come together.

He bounced his toe against the tightly woven edge of the red vintage rug underneath the table and nodded his head to an up-tempo rhythm.

Words, words, words. What words want to be in this song? No words? "Film," you want to be in the song, right? Who wants to join "film"? Anyone? Any words? How about you, "xilm"? Gah! Still not a word.

He'd been racking his brain all day for lyrics—in school, on the soggy walk home, and just now, while airing up the tires in the backyard. Will must have had some sort of conscience, since he'd only let the air out rather than slashing them. Either that, or he didn't have a pocketknife.

Could he write a song about a bully without a pocketknife? Maybe. Was that something he'd want to send to Corinne? Probably not.

Geoff sighed and stared at the old light fixture above the dining room table. None of the songwriting tricks he'd learned were working. He'd tried observing the world around him, like various things around the room, thinking about the word "film," and also . . . looking at things around the room.

It was possible he'd been reading the wrong books on songwriting.

He paced into the living room and looked out the front window to the street. Maybe there was something there that would inspire him. *Let's see . . . pavement, rain, grass. Any of y'all want to be in a song? No? What about you, porch? Alright, I'll come back to you later.*

So, no inspiration from outside; check. Geoff wandered around the main floor of the bungalow, which wasn't much of a trip. Just an entryway, a living room, a dining room, a kitchen, his dad's room, a bathroom, and his dad's study.

One of those things wasn't like the other, and it wasn't the bathroom even though having a toilet was a pretty distinguishing feature. Geoff wasn't really allowed in his dad's study. It wasn't a hard and fast rule, but it was certainly implied.

Maybe he'd just take a quick peek into his dad's inner sanctum. There were tons of things in there that might spark inspiration. Including that old book his dad kept trying to keep from him. What was the deal with that thing?

Only one way to find out.

He took a bite of the apple and wandered into his dad's study.

There hadn't been much to the room when they first moved in. Crazy what a few bookcases, a desk, and a dark green Tree of Life carpet could do to a place. His dad had a knack for finding things secondhand and curating them as though they lived in a museum.

Much like his store, the shelves were stuffed with old books but also displayed some vintage taxidermy, like a raven whose eyes seemed to follow you regardless of where you were in the room. There were jars full of curiosities, like weird-looking bones and tools. Tiny sculptures stood sentry like a gang of misfit toys prepared to report any suspicious activity. Some were carved from wood, some from jade, while others were delicate, ornate, and made of porcelain. When he was younger, Geoff had had a recurring dream that one of the carvings, a little wooden gnome dressed in green overalls and a tiny red stocking cap, would visit his room in the middle of the night. Just crack open the door and stare at him.

At least, he was 99 percent sure those were dreams.

Thankfully, he hadn't had one of those since they'd moved to Portland. Maybe he was outgrowing nightmares like that, or maybe the little gnome couldn't navigate the steep, spiraling staircase to the attic. Either way, he was glad to have the experience behind him.

Of course, Geoff knew he wouldn't find the book on any of those shelves. His dad would have kept it out of sight based on his reaction earlier that morning. So, where would it be?

His dad's study looked like the type of place that would have a secret room behind a bookcase that you could only enter if you pulled the right book or tweaked the wing of the taxidermied raven. But considering they'd just moved into the house, and Geoff had seen the original layout, there probably wasn't anything more to investigate on that front.

The professor had ordered a particular brand of old safe from the 1800s. Geoff remembered his dad saying that no fae would touch that specific type of iron, no matter how powerful.

You'd think a lifetime growing up with his dad would make hearing things like that less strange, but you'd be wrong. Thankfully, he was still dealing with some logistical issues related to delivering something that heavy to a house instead of someplace with a lift gate—whatever that was.

So, really, that only left one place to look—the middle drawer of his dad's desk, underneath a bunch of scattered junk.

His old man was funny like that. A planner, for sure. But all his plans had to be just so. He would eventually find the perfect place to secure it and other artifacts like it, but in the meantime, he'd put about as much thought into it as a squirrel hiding a pecan under a bunch of dead leaves.

Geoff slumped into the leather-tufted roller chair behind his dad's desk and rubbed the palm of his hand across the worn patina of its weathered oak top. He scooted the chair back to make room enough to open the drawer and rifled through a bunch of loose papers. Some were notes in his dad's pristine cursive writing that Geoff could barely read. He wondered when they'd stopped teaching that style of writing in school. His dad had tried to teach him at various points throughout his life, but Geoff had never really caught on. No one ever used it, so what was the point?

There was an old advertisement for a place called Keen's Magic Shoppe: "Our prices are so low that now you see them, and now you don't!" Geoff continued to filter through odds and ends and gently lifted some old pencil sketches of supernatural creatures doing menial tasks, like a djinn working the checkout at Home Depot, until he finally found what he was looking for.

There you are.

There was a bolt to his heart, almost like when someone jumps out from behind a couch when you're not ready, but he wasn't scared, and it didn't surprise him. It was something else. Like a cousin to that feeling. And there was that gravity again. That pull that the book had on him.

Geoff glanced around the room as though someone may have been watching him, which was highly unlikely. His dad wouldn't be back for at least another hour, but he couldn't shake the feeling. Maybe it was just the weird raven, but what if it was that gnome?

Ugh. That gnome creeps me out worse than the gremlin.

He exhaled before easing the blood-red tome from the drawer to set it on the desk. He ran his fingers along the carvings that someone had spent hours, maybe days, etching.

Geoff had seen a bunch of his dad's books lying around, but none of them really interested him. He'd actually read a couple of magic books before, but those were mostly on card tricks and how to make it look like you'd cut a rope in two when you actually just had two pieces of rope. This certainly wasn't that type of book. If he'd ever seen a book that held the secrets of real magic, then this was it.

The leather creaked as he gingerly opened the front cover. He was careful not to crease the spine or leave any markings his dad might notice later. He stared at the title page, which was written in thick, cursive calligraphy. He leaned in closer and then further away, hoping the varying perspective would give him a clue as to what the book was titled, but without any luck.

He rubbed his hands together. *Why are my hands sweating? It's just a book. I probably won't even be able to read it if the rest of it is written like this.*

There was something about the pages. They had a unique feel and sound that they made as he turned them. One moment the paper felt as brittle as a moth's wings, the next like a thin, pliable leather. He carefully leafed through a few blank pages until he reached the table of contents, which, mercifully, was printed in solid block letters.

There was the foreword, blah blah blah, "Basics of Practice," blah blah, "Dark Omens," "Light Omens," "When and How to Build a Crow Army," "Occult Accounting," "How to Cleanse Your Room of Evil Spirits" . . . blah blah blah . . . "Wish Fulfillment."

"Wish Fulfillment"? What if this is real? What if Dad isn't some weird dude obsessed with magic because it's his job or something? What if I could actually wish for something?

No, that's ridiculous.

Geoff glanced around the room. "Stop looking at me, raven."

What do I have to lose, here, five minutes? Besides, experiences like these can make for good songs; maybe I can write about this. OK, guess we're doing this. Here goes nothing. Literally. Nothing is going to happen.

Geoff sighed and went back to the table of contents.

Oh my god, there are like seventeen chapters on different ways to make a wish. Which one should I choose? They wouldn't just put the best one in the front, would they? They'd probably make you work for it, hide it in the middle somewhere. Like how you're always supposed to guess C on multiple-choice tests if you don't know the answer.

He chose a chapter from the middle of the wish stack and hungrily flipped through the oddly textured parchment.

Beware, dear reader, and know thyself. Making and living out a wish is a dangerous affair, not for the weak of mind, body, or spirit—

Blah, blah, blah. If this actually worked, it would be exactly what he needed for his date with Corinne. No, for his song. No, not for that, either.

He should wish for something great like his dad always told him. He should wish for two billion dollars.

. . . This is not a recipe for immediate wealth in the conjuring of cash or coin . . .

OK, he thought. The two billion dollars were off the table, so he'd just wish for the song. But wait, why wish for a song when he could just wish to get the girl?

. . . or love. Magic is the manipulation of elements of nature, not the strongest unseen tie known to man.

But why wouldn't he just wish to move back to Houston? If he could wish for anything, that would be a good wish. But would the spell know what part of Houston to move him back to? Besides, there wasn't anyone like Corinne back there. There wasn't anyone like Corinne anywhere, she was one of one, and he had a challenge to meet if he wanted any chance with her.

Fine then, the song it was. He'd wish for an unforgettably hooky, upbeat banger that no one could deny was good even if they didn't like it.

Geoff scanned the chapter. There was a grocery list of items he'd need in order to cook up a potion.

He pinched the bridge of his nose and stared at the ceiling. There was no way he had time to ride his bike to the store and back before his dad got home. *Maybe there's a wish for more time . . . no, Geoff. Focus.*

After scanning the list, he was pretty sure they had everything he needed in the house. One of the advantages of having a kooky dad was having a pantry full of bonkers ingredients like eye of newt around. Which, fun fact, is a reference to a mustard seed, not an actual lizard's eyeball, because that would be gross.

He tiptoed into the kitchen, using a finger as a temporary bookmark between the pages before carefully placing it on the counter. He held his palms featherlight against either side of the open book as though he was worried it would float away.

Why am I sneaking around? No one is here.

Geoff slid out the built-in spice rack next to the microwave above the stovetop.

Let's see, adder's tongue, adder's tongue . . . that's a plant, not a snake part, right? Yeah, there it is. He grabbed a small cork-topped bottle and set it aside.

Am I doing this because I think this is going to work, or am I just taking this opportunity to procrastinate? Geoff grabbed a bottle of allspice. "Huh," he said out loud. "I guess it really goes with everything."

Procrastination or not, we're doing this.

The instructions said to boil the ingredients in a cast iron cauldron, but the only cauldrons they had—and to be sure, Geoff's dad definitely kept cauldrons—were either hilariously small or cracked and damaged in some way that made them unusable.

They did, however, have an old cast iron skillet, which was close enough. Hopefully.

The bad news was that Geoff wasn't allowed to use it. Something about ruining the seasoning? However, he was already on a trust-breaking roll by snooping through his dad's stuff and reading a book his dad did not want him to touch, so what was one more tiny little infraction?

He sank into a crouch as he dug through the cabinet to pull out the skillet and fired up the electric range. Geoff's dad had thought it would be a good idea to replace the old gas range with electric since their house had solar panels. "Who puts solar panels on a house in Portland?" Geoff remembered asking his dad.

"Quiet, you," his dad responded.

What would Merlin think about using an electric range to cook up a potion instead of a flame? Would it set him to spinning in his grave? If some accounts were to be believed, maybe he would be spinning alive, since he had been entombed in rock by Nimue.

Long story and beside the point.

Either way, Geoff was using the tools at his disposal and entertained the possibility that Merlin would be so impressed by electricity that he'd use it almost exclusively.

The book's instructions required an incantation once the magical recipe came to a simmer. Geoff read it through a couple of times while silently practicing the rhythm of the words in a language whose time was long past. He couldn't help but wonder why all magic spells seemed to be in Latin. Why did mystical language refuse to evolve? Why couldn't it be translated into modern English, or Spanish, or whatever? Wouldn't it all mean the same thing?

Focus, Geoff, you only have a limited window of time to do this. Dad will be home soon.

He took a deep breath and shook out his hands. Why was he so nervous? Did he actually believe this would work?

Yeah, he kinda did.

He closed his eyes and held a hand above the steaming skillet. The vapor felt like it seeped through his skin and into his bloodstream. As though magic raced through the veins of his arm to his heart, which then pumped the spell out to the rest of his body.

He leaned forward, wafted the water vapor into his nostrils, and felt a similar effect in his lungs. There was a crackling energy deep within his chest that tingled out to his nerve endings, raising the tiny hairs along his arms.

Something inside Geoff crept forward and whispered that it was time to recite the incantation.

He didn't have to read from the page. The words were stamped into his mind's eye like subtitles on a French film. However, what came out of his mouth didn't sound like the words in his mind's eye. In fact, the words in his mind's eye didn't even look like words.

They were in hieroglyphs that he could only momentarily understand.

All he could hear coming out of his mouth was sounds like someone talking underwater—all bubbles and gibberish.

Now! Wish now! his mind cried out, or maybe it was his soul, somewhere or something deep within himself that was desperate to say the words in time with some sort of musical arrangement he couldn't hear. He focused his will to wish for a song with a hook no one could forget. A song with a legitimate rhyme for "film"—a real word that people used.

His stomach felt like it was boiling. Like he was a human teakettle. Only instead of whistling, he screamed, "One, two, three, four!" like a drummer counting off an intro.

The lights flickered and failed.

Or did they? Geoff realized he was squeezing his eyelids shut tight. Maybe that would explain the darkness. He relaxed his eyes and blinked. *Nope, the lights are definitely out.*

Maybe it was a neighborhood power outage? He looked out the kitchen window. *No, the Myers's lights are on. Did I just do magic? Do you do magic? What do you call it when you successfully perform a magic spell? Oh my god, why is it so hard to catch my breath right now?*

The lights overhead returned to their former brightness.

Do lights do that? I thought you had to reset the breaker after an outage.

Geoff moved the skillet off the burner and turned off the heat. He stretched his arms wide as though he'd just woken up from a refreshing afternoon nap. *Wow, I feel pretty good right now.*

For the first time since the move, Geoff felt in place. No longer were his feet in Portland while his heart remained in Houston. He was finally of one mind and body.

And he knew precisely what needed to come next.

He jogged up the winding staircase to his room and flopped into a purple midcentury-modern chair next to the tiny white desk he'd picked out at an estate sale with his dad. He flipped open his laptop, tuned his guitar, and tested his mic. "Rock test, one. Rock test, two." The volume gauge ran green as he strummed his guitar a couple of times. You wanted it green. If it seeped into yellow occasionally, that was fine, but never red. You'd be distorting at red, and unwanted distortion was bad. "Alright, let's do this," he said to himself. Geoff dialed in the BPM for the AI-assisted drummer and hit record.

Let's go to a movie,
Let's go see a film,
Nothing rhymes with that word,
So, I'll invent one: GILM!
GILM! GILM! GILM!
It's totally legitimate.
GILM! GILM! GILM!
Yeah, everybody's saying it.
It could be a verb,

Or it could be a noun,
And everybody's saying it, all around the town.

The words poured out of him. Even after the first pass, he felt like he had it. He just needed to add some bass, background vocals, and a lead guitar part. The whole process was over in half an hour.

GILM! Could he use a word he'd invented? Corinne had clearly stated that it had to be a real word that people used, no dead languages and all that. But unlike "xilm," "pilm," and all the other nonsense words he'd discarded, "GILM!" felt like it meant something.

It could mean anything.

Maybe it was the magic, or maybe it was irrational confidence, but either way, he was sending it. A blue bar ran across his browser as he uploaded the file to SoundCloud.

Geoff leaned back in his chair and let out a sigh. For once, everything was going his way. Nothing could ruin this moment.

Thunk!

Except for the sound of that car door. Or, more specifically, a sprinter van door.

Dad is home. He gripped the corners of the chair's armrests. *I left everything out in the kitchen! He is going to murder me with disappointment.*

The Unusual Effects

Geoff's dad wasn't the type to fly off the handle and yell. Instead, he would stay calm, fold his arms, and politely convey his disappointment through sullen eyes and bushy, furrowed eyebrows.

Which was somehow worse.

It's satisfying to get mad back at someone who's yelling. It's an appropriate, reflexive response. However, it's extremely difficult to be angry in retaliation to disappointment. At least Geoff hadn't figured out a way yet.

Geoff wasn't great at math, but suddenly, he became a physics wunderkind as he mentally modeled a series of calculations concerning his dad's path from the car. There was a short walk from the street to the house, then a stop at the mailbox and the sorting of mail before unlocking the front door. From there, he usually headed to either his study or the kitchen. That gave Geoff anywhere from thirty seconds to a minute.

So that begged the question, where should he cover his tracks first?

He knew his dad was super protective of the weird old book, so Geoff bounded down the stairs as quickly as possible to snatch it from the kitchen counter and return it to its original location in his dad's desk drawer.

His foot slipped in some of the spillage from the spell's ingredients, and he momentarily lost his grip on the book.

He was like a spy in an action movie, elegantly sliding under a security laser to avoid detection, but in a hapless and clumsy way that wasn't anything like a scene from that type of movie.

Thankfully, the book was moving at the same rate of speed as he was, so when he fell, it landed harmlessly on top of him.

Geoff held his breath as he checked the book for a bent spine or creased page. Everything looked fine, but he didn't have time to examine it further.

The leather soles of his dad's oxfords clapped against the wooden steps as he made his way up from the street below.

Geoff stayed low and undetectable as he scurried into his dad's office.

Their mailbox hung beside their front door, and the rusty clank of its lid signaled his dad was only seconds away from entering the house.

Geoff didn't have much time. He prayed the letter carrier had brought an exciting envelope or two. Maybe a catalog of tweed jackets or a Tim Burton collectibles auction to distract his dad and buy him a few more seconds.

He arranged the papers in the drawer like a crime scene analyst. Each piece of junk needed to go back into its precise spot if he wanted to remain a free man. After all, what good would it do for him to successfully conjure a spell for a date with Corinne, only to be grounded for the rest of his high school career?

The key slid into the lock, and the latch snatched open. There was no time left to cover up the evidence in the kitchen.

Think, think, think.

Geoff hurried to the bathroom, which, while it wasn't the kitchen, wasn't his dad's study either. He could probably make his dad believe the stove was a mess because he'd made a snack rather than because he'd cast a spell to impress a girl.

Whether or not the book was actually magic, the breach of trust Geoff had created by going through his dad's personal items was way worse than failing to properly clean and stow the professor's cast iron skillet.

The door shut, and he could hear the professor striding toward the dining room.

OK, what does a casual exit from the bathroom look like? Wipe hands on pants, turn off the lights . . . maybe yawn?

"You tired?" His dad tossed his leather satchel down on one of the dining room chairs and unwound the scarf from around his neck. Geoff's dad wore scarves. Most people in the Pacific Northwest wouldn't dare, but the professor somehow managed to pull off the look.

"No," Geoff said.

"What's that smell?"

"The bathroom," Geoff said, almost like a question.

"The bathroom," his dad repeated. He didn't seem convinced. "OK. How was school?"

"Fine."

"Homework done?"

"Not yet."

"What have you been doing?"

"Nothing."

His dad rolled his eyes. "Doesn't smell like nothing."

"I made a snack."

His dad's eyes narrowed. "So, is that smell a snack or the bathroom?"

Dang it, he's good. He could have been a lawyer. Maybe I can ignore the question and he won't notice. "I was just about to clean up in there," Geoff said.

"That my cast iron skillet?"

Geoff's stomach dropped. *Here we go.* "Uh, yeah. I was reading about how it makes stuff taste better when you cook it in one. Especially one that's well seasoned."

"OK," his dad said. He glanced from Geoff's face to the skillet, then back again.

He's not buying it. What can I say that's most believable?

His dad waved his hand dismissively. "Just make sure to rinse it, no soap. Thin coat of olive oil and throw it into the oven for twenty minutes at four hundred degrees. Can you do that?"

"Yeah, I've seen you do it."

"Good. I'm going to tie up some loose ends in my study. You going to be hungry for dinner in a little bit?"

"Yeah."

His dad shook his head. "I wish I had your metabolism."

"OK," Geoff said, and made his way toward the kitchen, minding every step for normalcy, which made him feel even more abnormal. How did he usually walk? What was a casual gait? How did he know "gait" meant "the style in which one walks"?

The catch to his dad's study door clicked, and Geoff exhaled a sigh of relief as long as his school's lunch line on pizza day. He never understood why that line was so long, though. School pizza was terrible.

As Geoff rinsed the pan and oiled it up while waiting for the oven to come to temperature, he realized he'd been humming his new song the entire time. It was catchy. Really catchy. Which, of course, it would be if the old book was worth anything.

He crossed his arms and leaned against the kitchen counter. *I can't believe I just got away with that.*

The door to the study flew open. Startled, Geoff hit his head on the edge of the cabinet. He sucked air through his teeth and rubbed the back of his head, partly to soothe himself, but mostly to make sure he wasn't bleeding.

His dad emerged in the kitchen doorway in rolled-up sleeves. He looked Geoff up and down. "Go do your homework."

The Green Room

Geoff stared at the history assignment on his computer screen, but his mind was elsewhere. He couldn't help but imagine what it would be like walking into Mr. Dent's classroom the next morning. Would Corinne's grazel gaze be one of anticipation, excitement, or disappointment?

He vacillated between victory and catastrophe before managing to tear his mind away from the anxiety loop and focus back on homework.

He cranked "GILM!" to see how it sounded to him after a few listens. Would it keep his attention? Would he hate it? Would he like it even more?

He breezed through his homework and realized he'd probably listened to the song a dozen times but wasn't getting tired of it. He'd created it less than an hour ago and could hardly believe it came from him.

He didn't put as much faith in mysticism as his father, but maybe there was something to it. Or maybe it was like a sense-memory focus shift, like poets or writers who light incense or candles to get into a creative frame of mind. Flow state, they called it.

He cruised through English and physics before hearing a knock at the bottom of the stairs. The door hinges creaked, and his dad called up, "Are you ready to eat?"

Geoff was always ready to eat. "Yeah, be right down."

His dad must have popped over to the taco shop down the street, because there were takeout boxes and plates on the table, and that kind of layout didn't just magically appear.

Or did it? Now that Geoff had potentially been exposed to the existence of magic in his life, anything was possible.

Geoff loaded his plate with chicken verde tacos and cracked open a can of black cherry sparkling water— which initially sounded gross to him but wasn't. It reminded him of Dr Pepper.

"What was that song you kept playing up there?"

"'GILM!,'" Geoff said through chews of chicken taco.

"It's catchy."

"Thanks."

"That's you?"

"Yeah."

"When did you do that?"

"This afternoon."

"You're getting good."

"Thanks."

"Really good."

"Thanks."

"I love and value our conversations," his dad said.

"Ha," Geoff replied. He plowed through the rest of his tacos and noticed his dad was absent-mindedly humming his tune while drumming his fingers against the table's edge. The man seemed really into it.

Geoff grabbed his plate and stood up from the table. "Thanks for dinner, Dad. I love those tacos. I miss Tex-Mex, but whatever that is works fine for me."

"What?" His dad furrowed his brow and seemed to struggle to return his focus to the real world. "Oh. Yeah, tacos are good. Make sure to put your plate in the dishwasher," he said before zoning back out while humming the song.

Geoff grinned as he put away his dish and tossed his can into the recycling. *This song must be legitimately good.* Usually when Geoff's dad listened to one of his songs, he'd nod along, put on an exaggerated smile, and say, "This is good," in a really high voice that let Geoff know it wasn't that good.

He couldn't wait to share the link with Corinne and drummed his fingers along the wall as he jogged upstairs. He listened to "GILM!" a few more times to make sure it was perfect before firing off the link.

He slumped back into his seat and focused on his homework, periodically checking to see if she'd read his message.

No luck.

Once he'd finished all his assignments, he checked again, but again was only met with a delivered message instead of the desired *read.*

Could have been worse, though. It would have been way worse if it just said read with no reply.

He took a shower to pass some time, flossed as slowly as he could, and matched his tooth brushing cycle to the full length of "GILM!" *Surely she's had enough time to check by now.*

But she hadn't. *Delivered* remained under his text. He slid into the sheets and leaned back against the headboard. His mental math wunderkind was back modeling multiple scenarios. Maybe she lost her phone. Maybe the cell towers were down in her neighborhood. Maybe she did something that made her parents take her phone away as punishment.

What if she has read receipts turned off. Are mine turned off? Geoff checked his settings. Nope, they were showing for him. Wait, *what if my messages just aren't refreshing?*

He closed out the text app, reopened it, and brought up her text thread.

Read.

Yes.

Three dots appeared.

Then disappeared.

Then appeared again.

Then disappeared.

A minute went by. Then five.

No.

Then ten.

No . . . no.

Then twenty.

Oh my god. She thinks it sucks. Wait, what if this was a setup all along? What if she knew it would suck and just wanted to share it with all her friends from the musical? Like, "This guy hates musicals so much because he is bad at music. Just listen to how bad. Now send it to your friends, and they'll send it to their friends." I'm going to go viral for all the wrong reasons.

The Spotlight

Geoff's phone blared like a red alert. In three swift motions, he turned off the alarm and swiped into his messages.

Read.

No reply.

This is bad. This is really bad.

Geoff wondered what the best outfit would be to wear to his own funeral. Because that was what he would be riding his bike to that morning.

He sniffed a vintage graphic tee from an old movie called *Sky High* from the pile of clothes next to his dresser. He'd bought it from a thrift store because it was the Japanese version of the poster art, and he thought it looked cool. At least he hoped it was from the movie poster and didn't say *The guy wearing this shirt is an idiot* or something like that. The way things were going, he wouldn't be surprised. He threw a flannel over it and slid into his favorite pair of jeans. He might as well be comfortable if he was about to go through the worst day of his life.

He shuffled downstairs to the kitchen, where his dad poured a cup of coffee.

"Want some?" his dad asked.

He'd never offered Geoff coffee before.

"Sure."

He handed Geoff a cup, then poured the rest into his thermos. "So, 'GILM!' I feel like I know what it means, but I thought I'd ask you to make sure. Like, how is that coffee, is it GILM!?"

What is he talking about? Is he serious? "Yeah, Dad. This coffee is totally GILM!."

"I can't wait to GILM! my on-campus colleagues all about it today."

Geoff chuckled. "OK, Dad, take it easy."

"Welp, GILM! you later!" The professor screwed on the lid to his thermos and marched toward the front door.

"Yeah, Dad, GILM! you too."

Geoff's eyes darted sideways, and he felt his jaw drop. What was that all about? His dad acted strange sometimes, but usually in a dad-joking or a clutch-a-weird-book-tightly-and-not-talk-about-it kind of way. Geoff glanced at the clock and realized he would be late if he didn't get moving.

But why didn't Dad say something? He's always telling me I'm about to be late.

* * *

Geoff rolled up to the bike rack at an angle that put him as far away from Will as possible. He hunched his shoulders and did everything he could to make himself as small and unnoticeable as possible.

"Hey, Ge-off!" Will said. He pronounced it with a hard G.

Geoff did his best to ignore him.

"I said, hey, Ge-off," Will said in a surprisingly even tone of voice as he walked toward him.

"It's Geoff, Will," Geoff said, pronouncing his name with a soft G. "Like GIF."

"I know you mean the peanut butter," Will said. "Because the other thing stands for 'graphics interchange format.'"

Sometimes it was hard being a Geoff with a G instead of a J, so the whole GIF-versus-JIF pronunciation debate meant a lot to the Geoff community. It was important to him. He just couldn't believe Will knew what "GIF" stood for, and it threw him for a loop. So, he just stood there. Like a Geoff in headlights.

"I heard your song, Ge-off," Will said.

Geoff's hands froze on his handlebars. *Here we go . . .*

"It's pretty good."

Is he being sarcastic or real?

Geoff searched for a tone of voice that would indicate both a) he got the joke Will had just made, and b) simple and respectful acknowledgment. "Thanks, Will."

"You're welcome, Ge-off. Have a GILM! morning."

GILM! morning? What the heck? Geoff's world seemed to wobble. *What just happened? How did Will hear the song? Do I really want to know?*

Yeah, kinda.

"Hey!" Geoff yelled at Will. He couldn't believe he was voluntarily engaging with this guy.

Will spun around and arched an eyebrow. "Yeah?"

"How'd you hear my song?"

"My sister."

Huh. It would be funny if his sister is Corinne.

And by "funny," he meant "not funny at all." Like a total shit show on top of what was already a disaster. The girl Geoff had a crush on, who, for the past ten hours or so, he'd been catastrophizing as a potential cyberbully, as the sister of his real-life bully who might not actually be his bully anymore? Confusing. Either way, Geoff had to know.

"Who's your sister?"

"Corinne," Will said.

Of course she's his sister. GILM!, he thought. Wait, was he saying it now? What did that word even mean? It came out of him so fluidly that he felt like he knew what it meant. Weird that the word didn't mean anything before yesterday afternoon, but now it kind of meant everything.

"Also, don't touch her, Ge-off, or I'll GILM! you up."

The word really could mean anything. But Geoff was still pretty sure Will didn't have to worry when it came to him and Corinne. His fate was already sealed.

Geoff tugged on his bike lock to make sure it was secure while Will stood in the distance staring at him.

"I mean it," Will said, pointing his finger toward Geoff. The finger synchronized with the others in a curled fist. "GILM!," he said as he punched the fist into his other hand and then marched off toward the school, although he probably wasn't going in.

It didn't seem as dark outside as it had yesterday, or the day before, and certainly the weeks before. The sky was an incredible mix of orange and purple. Geoff wasn't a big look-at-the-sky kind of guy, but there he was, admiring it.

The lawn under his feet was firm instead of spongy from all the rain. If Geoff hadn't already known of the ridicule that awaited him inside, he'd have thought things were looking up for him.

The hallways were cluttered as usual, but for some reason, the crowd flow seemed to work in his favor that morning. It was as though the school couldn't wait to get him to his first class and his seat next to Corinne. Where, at best, he'd be met with an awkward silence from a girl who'd left him on read, or at worst, face the hungry eyes of a class full of scavengers starving for dead meat.

The first bell sounded, and the halls began to thin as people filed into their classrooms. He passed the musical sign-up sheet, which today felt more like a dark omen in high definition rather than the non-descript landmark in his peripheral vision.

OK, Geoff, you've been through worse. Well, you haven't, but you've been through bad things, and you always get past it. Besides, it's only a couple years until graduation, and you can always move far, far away from here, never to return. I hear Florida is nice.

He took a deep breath and crossed the threshold into Mr. Dent's class.

Every seat was filled except Geoff's, and almost every eye seemed trained on him. Of course they were. It was obvious that Corinne had sent his song out to everyone she knew.

His saliva retreated to the back of his throat, leaving his mouth dry while simultaneously almost choking him with his own spit.

He couldn't swallow in front of the entire class, though, right? Not with every eye on him like that; he'd look nervous. But he couldn't look nervous. He needed to project strength despite the fact that his saliva was building up like a river crashing against a crumbling dam.

Be cool. You just need to make it to your seat.

Geoff seemed to forget how to walk. He was now self-conscious about every single move. Which foot did he normally lead with? Should he swagger into the room or just walk upright and rigid? Because at that moment, he was definitely walking upright and rigid.

Geoff wanted to ask why everyone was looking at him, but he knew.

His hip caught the edge of one of the desks as he turned the corner to his row. He didn't know the girl who sat there, but now he'd never forget her voice.

"Are you OK?" she asked.

Of course he wasn't OK, but it was nice of her to ask. He'd remember her for her kindness. Good ol' what's-her-name.

He wanted to say thanks. But since his throat was still full of spit that he refused to swallow, he just turned, barely raised his hand above waist level, and made some weird froglike sound that he would also remember for the rest of his life.

Maybe he should have just wished to be a frog at this point. No one sees a frog and wants to hurt it. Everyone is delighted by the sight of a frog. Everyone. Maybe that wasn't true, but Geoff was thankful for the momentary mental distraction, so much so that he involuntarily swallowed the backed-up deluge of spit.

Which made him cough.

He hunched over into a minor coughing fit as he fell into the seat of his desk.

"Are you OK?" Corinne asked.

Am I OK, Corinne? I don't know, maybe. Maybe I'll choke to death on this spit I accidentally swallowed, but for now I'm trying to breathe like some sort of delightful frog and be done with this literal hellscape of a day where everyone is making fun of me because you made me look like a fool in front of the entire school, who I don't know but now knows me.

"I liked your song," Corinne said.

Liked my song, whatever, you two-faced . . . wait a minute. She sounds like she means it. Geoff had been avoiding her gaze but decided to throw caution to the wind and look her in the grazel eye. She seemed sincere. Actually, she seemed concerned. Geez, how bad was he coughing?

"Thanks," Geoff said. "I wasn't sure what you thought since I didn't hear from you. I'm glad you liked it." *Yeah, that sounded nice. Not insecure or anything, hopefully.*

"You didn't get my message?"

I got three dots. Did she mean to send me a message? Wait, did she share my song because she actually liked it?

Geoff shook his head. He pulled out his phone to show her the message, or rather the lack thereof, when—

"Mr. Smith!" Mr. Dent exclaimed. "Where do we put our phones once the bell rings?"

Oh no. He's going to take my phone and read my one-way message with Corinne, or maybe worse.

Mr. Dent had a known hatred of phones in the classroom. It was rumored that he had once been vice principal but was demoted after he took a student's phone and shattered it against a set of lockers during the homecoming dance.

The bell rang.

Geoff's chest inflated with hope. He might get off on a technicality since the phone was out before the official start of class. He tried not to smile. Smiling might set the guy off. It was always best to avoid enraging a man so tightly wound that you could put him into an old wristwatch and power it for the next fifty years.

"Alright, Mr. Smith," Mr. Dent said. "Put it away."

As Mr. Dent turned and approached the dry-erase board, a small, folded-up piece of paper hit the top of Geoff's desk. He glanced over to Corinne, who looked straight ahead but was doing a terrible job of hiding a tight-lipped smile.

Geoff unfolded a torn piece of printer paper around the size of a dollar bill.

Thought I'd try out your pen-and-pad routine. It's kind of fun, although how do you delete your mistakes? Haha, just kidding. Pizza tonight, I know just the spot. Be ready by six o'clock. Text me your address, and I'll pick you up. But not right now, Dent is watching. In fact, eat this note so he can't take it from you and read it to the class.

Geoff grinned and kept one eye on Dent. He cautiously turned to get a look at Corinne. She responded with an eating motion and a thumbs up.

Geoff shrugged and crumpled the note as quietly as he could. Luckily, his hands were so sweaty it helped soften the paper and avert any crinkling sounds. He looked around to ensure no one but Corinne could see him before darting the paper into his mouth like a bearded dragon snatching a cricket.

Her jaw dropped.

Why is she looking at me like that?

The Secret
of the Song

The bell rang, and the classroom sprang to life like someone had kicked the top off of an anthill. Everyone seemed to have had enough of Dent's lecture and was ready for whatever came next.

"I was just joking about eating the note," Corinne said as she slid her tablet into her backpack.

"Then why did you make the eating gesture?"

"Because I'm taking you for pizza later, Geoff. Oh my god."

"Oh yeah." Geoff jammed his notebook into his backpack and zipped it up quickly. He wanted to keep pace with Corinne as long as he could until their next class. "Well, it was confusing."

"Now we'll never have our first note for the scrapbook." Her grazel eye stared at Geoff through strands of dark hair like an excited actor peeking through the curtain on opening night. She slid her backpack on and tossed her hair back over her shoulder.

"Don't worry, I know just the thing, give me a second." Geoff hunched over and made it look like he was going to throw up.

"Stop it, that's gross," Corinne said. "I don't

want that image in my head when I'm listening to my new favorite song."

Geoff still wasn't a hundred percent sure she wasn't messing with him, but at that point, he decided to just go with it. "You really like it, huh?"

"Yeah, it's GILM!"

"It's GILM!?"

"GILM!," she said as they strolled down either side of the aisle of desks. "Yeah, everybody's saying it."

Geoff didn't understand how or why Corinne, Will, and his dad were using "GILM!" as a substitute word that morning, but at least they were saying it. For the first time in his life, he'd done something that resounded with people.

It felt good. And it felt weird to feel good.

But was that why it felt weird, or was it something else?

Corinne hooked her arm around his and led Geoff out of the classroom. "You're going to love this place tonight. There's this one pizza with prosciutto, arugula, and a honey drizzle . . . so good."

"OK, but do they have pepperoni?" Geoff asked. "Because I'm kind of into pepperoni."

"Pepperoni? You can expand your horizons. I believe in you. Come on, try it."

"Corinne!" Two faces emerged from the mass of bodies in the hall: a guy and a girl decked out in the latest trend that Geoff not only would never wear but also could never afford. "Is this the 'GILM!' guy?" the girl asked.

"That's him," Corinne said. "Geoff, this is Mary—"

"*GILM! GILM! GILM!*" Mary exclaimed.

A couple of other voices in the hallway peppered in their own "GILM!"s.

Geoff had a hard time maintaining eye contact. *That seems like genuine enthusiasm. Now what do I do?* Maybe the only thing worse than no one paying attention to him was someone paying too much attention.

"Love the song, Geoff," the guy with Mary said. He made rock horns and shouted, "*GILM!!*" as he walked off. The word faded like a runaway train down the hall.

OK, Geoff thought. *That's more like it.* Faceless and distanced attention felt right.

Corinne led him through the hall with her arm in his. Geoff could not have imagined a greater moment in his life. Eyes shifted toward him instead of glazing, staring ahead, or actively averting. Hands shot to mouths to hide excited whispers as they passed.

"This is where I leave you," Corinne said. "Pick you up at six."

The eye contact was electric, and Geoff fought every instinct inside of him to look away. "I'll be ready. Excited to try your pizza salad or whatever."

Her eyes actually sparkled. He didn't realize people's eyes did that in real life.

As she faded into the mass of students in the hall, Geoff allowed himself to think things couldn't get any better than this. He turned to head to his next class, only to be confronted by another familiar face.

Her brother, Will. His eyebrows knitted together like two snakes squaring off in a territorial dispute. He squared his jaw and punched his right hand into his left.

When did Will start going to class?

The Interlude

The basketball team serpentined through the hallway like a wool-and-leather-sleeved dragon. Geoff acted like he was going one way, then slipped in beside them as they passed.

Will was pushing people aside to try to find him. Apparently, the tactic worked.

Geoff exhaled. He shrugged his backpack higher on his shoulder and stood a little taller.

"You the 'GILM!' guy?" someone from the team asked. According to his jacket, he was number twenty-four.

"Yeah, I guess I am the 'GILM!' guy."

"I put your song on our warm-up playlist," number twenty-four said.

What do I say to that? "Nice"? "Thanks"? Do I have a conversation? Is he going to get mad if I don't appreciate his gesture enough? This guy is huge. I wonder how long it would take him to knock me out. Like, one swing? Maybe. "Nice! Thank you," Geoff said.

"GILM!," number twenty-four said.

Geoff waved and peeled off from the basketball team as they approached his next class. Everyone inside stopped what they were doing and stared at him.

Is there something in my nose? Is my hair sticking out?

Geoff discreetly checked his fly. *Good, it's still up.*

"GILM! guy!" someone exclaimed.

The word bounced around the room from one person to the next. "GILM! GILM! GILM!."

Oh yeah, I'm the GILM! guy.

The school's starting quarterback, Jock Sampson or something—Geoff didn't exactly know his name—lumbered by at a massive six foot four.

"Good song," Jock said, and cuffed Geoff on the shoulder. "We listened to it in workout this morning. GILM!ed four more reps per set than usual. Definitely adding that to the playlist."

"Thanks," Geoff said as he slid into his seat.

"That's your song?" the girl in the seat next to him asked. She hadn't looked his way once the entire time they'd been in that class together. "The GILM! one?"

"Yeah."

She tapped the shoulder of the girl next to her. "He wrote 'GILM!.'"

"Yeah, Montanna," the girl said. "I know. Everyone knows, GILM!."

Geoff wasn't sure if she'd just used the word as an exclamation or a substitute for the word "duh," but either way, Geoff was enjoying the attention. But especially from Corinne. He couldn't wait for their date later that night.

He just needed to avoid her brother in the meantime.

The bell rang, and Mrs. Cartright closed the door to the classroom. "GILM! morning, class."

This is getting ridiculous.

Mrs. Cartright settled into her lesson about "imposter syndrome," a term for when successful people don't feel like they've earned their success. Geoff started to take notes, but his mind couldn't help but wander.

Could a spell from a book actually work? Was that a thing that could happen? Sure, he'd felt something happen last night, but wasn't that like getting goose bumps while watching a scary movie? It was all psychosomatic, right? It had to be.

What if his song was just really good?

He stared out the window. This was what he'd always wanted. To be known for something he'd created. To be understood on his terms. So, why did it feel so off?

Imposter syndrome.

That was it! That was what it was. Just what Mrs. Cartright was saying. Some people can't or won't feel their own success. Of course, it seemed a little grandiose to think of a few kids and a teacher quoting his song as success, but—wait. Was that imposter syndrome too? Or was that perfectionism? Thinking that your success isn't actually success.

Psychology is confusing.

Geoff zoned in and out for the rest of the period, and he seemed to only notice class was over once people were moving around him. He looked down at his notes, only to discover he'd sketched a pretty decent rendition of the old book from his dad's store.

It set him on edge. Something about the way it sat on the page felt menacing. But how could an inanimate object sit menacingly? Cats crouched, ready to pounce; owls stood, ready to swoop; but books were just supposed to sit.

Whatever, it's just a doodle on a page. A really good doodle, though. If I can keep this up I could create my own album artwork instead of using public-domain images.

He jammed his spiral-bound notebook into his backpack and made his way to the hallway. He could hear the boxy sound of a portable speaker in the crowd and noticed heads bopping along in unison, bringing order to the normally chaotic hallway.

Geoff squinted. The heads were nodding in unison to his song.

There was a group huddled together at a locker, some chatting, some dancing. He'd never seen anyone dance in the hallway before, not in real life, anyway.

Hands shot into the hair to emphasize the words in the chorus: *"GILM! GILM! GILM!"*

Again, Geoff thought he should feel better about this. It should have been his moment at the end of a movie after an hour and a half of angst and trouble while overcoming all odds to have his song sung by the entire school.

But instead, he felt unsettled.

Maybe it wasn't imposter syndrome at all, maybe he just didn't like success. Maybe he didn't like himself.

Why couldn't he be happy in his triumphant moment?

And why couldn't he stop thinking about that weird old book his dad brought home?

Bodies started scattering in the hallway.

"Ge-off!"

It was Will. Of course it was Will.

Geoff mentally scrambled for an escape, but this time the basketball team wasn't there to save him. His eyes darted, looking for any possible egress, before zeroing in on a target.

He shouldered through an unlocked classroom door and peered through the vertical rectangle of safety glass. Will's head and shoulders bobbed through the crowd like a sea lion floating through a kelp bed.

Are sea lions dangerous? Probably not important, but they have to be if someone branded them the ocean version of a lion instead of, like, a dog.

Will floated away in the hallway's sea of bodies, and Geoff exhaled a lungful of anxiety-infused air. He took a moment to collect himself before realizing he wasn't in this classroom alone. A teacher in an olive-green cardigan sat behind his desk. He mindlessly chewed gum while nodding his head along to the music playing through his earbuds.

Tinny air pushed out from the buds and into the room. *"GILM! GILM! GILM!"* The teacher didn't look up or acknowledge Geoff's presence in any way. He just stared into space with glazed eyes behind thick, chunky glasses, humming along to the music.

The crowd in the hall was starting to thin, which meant Geoff didn't have much time to get to class.

Whatever cover he'd had was no longer there to protect him from Will.

Geoff quietly twisted the doorknob and peered outside before he dashed down the hallway and up the staircase to his next class. He stopped at the top of the stairs and peeked around the brick-lined corner to make sure his path was clear. No one in the hall to the right, just two doors and about twenty feet to the classroom. However, to the left, about thirty feet away, was a set of sneakers angrily squeaking toward him.

Above the furious sneakers were irritated corduroys, which were just below a black T-shirt marked with the spiral letters of the name of a death metal band, which was just below the snarling mug of Corinne's brother, Will.

Geoff's heart pumped pure adrenaline as his "fight, freeze, or flee" instinct came in.

He chose flee.

His knees buckled at the takeoff of his sprint toward the door for English. Maybe all that adrenaline confused his body; Geoff wasn't sure, but he didn't have time to think about it.

He knew he didn't have to make it all the way into the class, he just needed to be in the line of sight of his teacher. Geoff pulled his shirt tight against his body with one hand and curled his backpack around to make it more difficult for a grabby hand to grasp.

A couple of seconds had never stretched so long.

The squeaks of Will's sneakers gained on him as the door to his classroom stood mere feet away.

A hand reached out.
From the classroom.
And curled around the door handle.
No. Don't close the door. No!

The Echo Pedal of Unexpected Side Effects

Fingertips grazed the back of Geoff's shirt. If his heart weren't beating like a metronome set to the BPM of abject terror, he would have smiled at the fact that his little shirt-tightening trick worked.

"No running," Ms. Henson called. "I said, no running!" Her eyes stayed glued to Will until he disappeared around the corner. "Kid even runs like a turd. If it weren't for his shoes, I'd have to call a janitor to mop the brown streaks off the floor."

Geoff tried to slow his breathing down, but it only made things worse.

"You OK?" she asked.

No. He was definitely not OK.

"I'm fine," Geoff said.

"If you say so," she said. "Everyone, find your seat."

Geoff slumped into his seat as the bell rang. He could feel the eyes trained on him, but this time, he understood. It was hard to ignore an entrance where someone was gasping for breath.

He pulled out his notebook and rummaged through another pocket in his bag for a pencil. He scrawled the date across the top right-hand corner of an empty page and breathed one last sigh through his nose.

"Eyes up here," Ms. Henson said. She stepped toward the whiteboard at the front of the beige-walled classroom. "Today, we will be deconstructing literature in the form of a modern poem." She uncapped her green dry-erase marker and began to write at the top of the board.

"I had a plan for us to examine a work by former poet laureate Tracy K. Smith. However, earlier this morning, I was inspired to change today's curriculum. Something has captured the zeitgeist of the school, so I think we should take a closer look."

She stepped away from the whiteboard to reveal the word "GILM!" underlined twice.

Oh my god, I'm going to be sick.

Ms. Henson put the cap back on the marker and rested it below her chin. "When the author proclaims, 'Let's go see a movie, let's go see a film,' what are they really saying?"

Hands shot up around the classroom.

Ms. Henson's eyes bulged as if she'd never seen class participation like this. She pointed to a paisley-dressed, chunky-booted girl in the front row. "Becca."

"I think he's expressing one's desire to escape their banal existence and take a moment to consider the possibility of something more. Witness an ensemble's tale told from a singular point of view."

I guess that's one way to put it. I never really thought of that. Is that what I meant?

Ms. Henson closed her eyes and meditated on the thought. "The singular point of view of a first-person narrator or the omniscient view of one who has pulled the story together from multiple points of view?"

Becca's eyes scanned the foam-tiled ceiling momentarily before returning to Ms. Henson. "My initial thought was first-person. Like a call to action, an invitation—'Let's go see a movie.' But after several listens, I think it is still an invitation, but from one on high, who sees all that gather below."

"Oh, interesting, Becca, well done," Ms. Henson said. "Kyle, you're next."

Hey, my nonfriend from Dad's store! This should be good.

Kyle shrugged off his cape and tented his fingers. "I think the movie is a metaphor," he said. Kyle straightened up taller and pivoted to address the room. "Sure, it's short for a motion picture or moving pictures, but to me, it represents a stagnant life and the desire for more. To me, 'Let's go see a movie' means 'let's go set our life in motion.' It's an invitation to us all to join the narrator in a life more fully lived."

Did "GILM!" just make him believe in friendship?

Applause dappled the room, and Kyle's hands met over his heart in a prayer salute. He bowed low and returned to his seat.

Ms. Henson thumbed tears away at the corner of each eye. "But, of course, we don't have to guess, do we?" She sniffed and straightened out the front end of her stylish knit sweater. "The author is with us today." She extended all five fingers, palm up, toward

Geoff with a full-faced grin that would have made the anchor of *Good Morning, Portland* jealous.

What am I supposed to say? That I just responded to a dare so I could go on a date with my crush?

Should I talk about the old book or lie and say I just sat down and wrote something off the top of my head without thinking about it? Should I just say "Write what you know and get out of your own way"? I've heard writers say that before.

It wasn't Geoff's worst nightmare, but it was close. His worst nightmare was still the little wooden gnome that stared at him through a crack of light in his barely-open door. Why did his dad even have that thing?

Anyway, public speaking sucked on a level just below that. Especially when Geoff knew he was going to say something stupid.

"Go ahead, Geoff." Ms. Henson gestured like she was easing a chicken into a backyard coop.

"Um," Geoff started.

"Speak up," said a voice in the back of the room.

"Yes," Ms. Henson said. "In fact, stand up so everyone can see and hear you."

Geoff stood and suddenly became very aware of his hands. *What did Kyle do with his? What do normal people do with their hands when they're talking? Should I do that finger-tenting thing in front of my midsection or the one-handed fisty-thumb-point thing for emphasis?* He jammed his hands into his pockets and rocked back and forth on his heels. "So, you know. The, uh . . . first line to any song is, like . . . a first impression."

"Very good point," Ms. Henson said. She wrote *first impression* on the whiteboard.

OK, so far, so good. Maybe I can just talk about the process, and she won't ask me anything more about what I meant. Step 1: have a weird dad. Step 2: find the strange book he hid in his desk drawer.

"So, what first impression are you trying to make here?" Ms. Henson asked.

Dang it.

"So," Geoff said, "I don't know if I was trying to make a first impression here."

"It's an invitation," Becca said, reiterating her point from earlier. "His first impression is that of inclusivity."

Thank you, Becca. I owe you.

"Yes!" Ms. Henson said. She was almost jumping with every stroke of the marker as she wrote *inclusivity*.

A girl in the front row stood. Her hair lay straight against her shoulders, and her bangs were cut in a perfect line above her eyebrows. "I think he's exploring the power dynamic in a post-capitalist society and how people can rally together against a system that's stacked against them."

Um, what?

"Interesting, Rachel." Ms. Henson scrawled *overthrow government/power back to the people/living wage for teachers.*

"GILM!," Rachel said.

Ms. Henson's face went from bright and animated to relaxed and dull. "GILM!," she replied.

"GILM!," the class responded in a monotone, unified voice.

Geoff slowly slid back into his seat. *What just happened? Why did they respond to the word like that? It's like they're hypnotized.*

Ms. Henson shook herself out of the daze, and the lively exchanges returned between her and his classmates for the next thirty minutes or so until the bell rang. He stared at the page of notes he had taken about his own song and couldn't believe the situation he'd found himself in. The thing he'd written wasn't his anymore. It was something else entirely.

But, had it ever been his? His time with the book felt like weeks ago, but it was only yesterday afternoon. More like a dream than a memory. What incantation did he even say out loud? Did his dad really bring home a magic book? Had all the stuff his dad had collected and sold over the years been legitimate, or was this the first thing?

His stomach felt sour.

The bell rang, and the classroom was set into motion. He closed his notebook and jammed it into his backpack as he stood to make his way toward the door. Ms. Henson was deep in conversation with Rachel and Kyle, no doubt talking about Geoff's song, but they didn't even bother to look up as he passed by. He couldn't hear exactly what they were saying, but it sounded like they were just repeating "GILM!" over and over to each other.

This was a mistake.

Geoff gave himself over to the flow of the river of students, which fed into the sea of the main hall. He searched for the current that would take him closest to the front doors. He wasn't sure if he was physically sick or if it was all just in his head, but either way, he needed to go home. If only to get another look at the book. No, not just get another look at it. He needed to destroy it. Maybe if the book ceased to exist, the spell would lose its power.

Maybe he should call his dad. No, that was the last thing he wanted to do. Geoff would rather have let the world fall into a chaotic refrain of "GILM!"s before telling his dad he'd been snooping around his office. Not that he'd blow up or anything.

Instead, he'd stay calm, fold his arms, and politely convey his disappointment through sullen eyes and bushy, furrowed eyebrows. Which, again, was somehow worse.

No, Geoff needed to come up with a plan on his own.

The cool outdoor air soothed the heat of his flushed cheeks as he trudged to the bike rack with a heaviness he'd never experienced before. Things weren't going according to plan, and he had to do something about it. The book was too dangerous to exist.

In the movies, if you kill the head vampire, then it releases all the other vampires from their curse. Or was it a werewolf? Maybe it was both. Whatever, if it worked for both or either, then surely if he burned the book, it would release the spell's hold on everyone.

Seeing Kyle again in class had reminded him of their exchange at his dad's store. Kyle mentioned that paper and ink couldn't stand up to water, which was true most of the time. But was that book even made of regular paper? It felt different, and as old as it was, what if the ink had sunk in to the point where it couldn't be erased, only smeared? There was no way a smudged word would be good enough to break the spell's hold.

Geoff decided instead to focus on his original inclination. His dad may have had a thing for the indelibly written word over electronics, but he'd have liked to see ink and page stand up to fire.

It was a good plan.

He turned the key to his bike's U-lock with authority and wound the chain just under the seat. He gripped the handlebars of his bike and kicked a leg over—

"Mr. Smith," Mr. Dent called.

Dang it. How did he see me? His classroom isn't anywhere near the front entrance.

The man practically leaned at a seventy-five-degree angle as he paced toward Geoff. He didn't know how he'd found himself on Dent's radar, but Mr. Dent had a knack for witnessing any time Geoff stepped a toe out of line. Literally. A couple of weeks ago, Geoff had been playing pickup basketball, and Dent had made them change the score because Geoff had a toe over the three-point line. What kind of person refs a random pickup game? A person who wears a tie with short sleeves even when it's forty-six degrees and drizzling outside. Mr. Dent.

"Principal's office, now!"

The Breakdown

Dent handed out detentions like he was on a quota, but sending someone straight to the principal's office just for being outside during school hours seemed extreme. Most teachers would have called out, "Back inside, mister," or something casual like that. Actually, most teachers were inside out of the rain. So, what was Dent doing out there?

Rumor had it Dent was gunning for the new vice principal's job (technically his old job if the whole cell phone rumor was true) since Mr. Johnson was retiring at the end of the year, so maybe he needed more face time with the boss.

Geoff sat hunched over in an old Danish modern chair just outside the principal's frosted glass door. He did not have time for this. That book had to go.

Should I burn it outside or inside? If I burn it inside, and it's magic, then it might explode or something. But what would the neighbors think if they saw me burning a book outside? Would they call the fire department, or just gossip about me for the next however many years as the kid who skips school to burn books?

The principal's secretary laughed at something Dent had said at a volume just low enough that Geoff couldn't hear. Mr. Dent stared at him as he leaned an elbow against the counter in the waiting room.

The secretary's grin dropped as her gaze scanned from Dent to Geoff. Her horned-rimmed glasses were straight out of a cartoon, but she somehow made it chic. People in this town had an uncanny sense of fashion.

"Wait," the secretary said. Her features softened as she slid the glasses down her nose. "Aren't you the 'GILM!' person?"

"'GILM!' guy," Geoff said, correcting her. It had already been a long day, and if they were going to laugh at him, he might as well make his own jokes.

"GILM!" she replied. It sounded more like a laugh than a word. She seemed to have a good sense of humor.

Unfortunately, Mr. Dent did not. Mirth was a zero-sum game for him.

"Watch it, Mr. Smith," Mr. Dent said. "That's another day's detention for you."

Another day? How many do I have coming?

"Sorry," Geoff said.

Geoff stared at the floor and squeezed his hands together. His fingers intertwined like he was in intense prayer. Which, in a way, he was. He would make a deal with anyone to have the last couple of days back. *Please, I will do anything to get out of this. Even sign up for Wicked. I don't care. Whatever you need, just please, please get me out of this.*

A bloopy alert sprang from the secretary's computer speaker. She adjusted her glasses and peered at the screen. "OK, Alexander, she's ready for you."

Of course Dent would be an Alexander. Not an Alex, not a Lex. Nope, all four syllables.

Dent spun like a Broadway actor stalking to center stage for his big scene. He paused for a moment, collected himself, and disappeared behind the frosted glass door.

Geoff casually leaned in the door's direction to try to catch whatever was said between the two in the office. It seemed like they were exchanging pleasantries, and the frosted outline of Mr. Dent took its seat.

Dent leaned back in the chair, seemingly in his element.

"First time in here?" the secretary asked.

Lady, I don't have time for small talk, I am trying to eavesdrop. Geoff composed himself as best he could. "Um, yes. First time."

"You'll be alright," she said.

She seemed kind, and although Geoff wanted to feel the relief she intended, his anxiety would not allow him a reprieve. He hadn't been in a principal's office since third grade, when he put a bunch of library books in his backpack without checking them out. He wasn't trying to steal them. He just didn't understand the process.

Anyway, none of that mattered. He had to find a way out of there and back to the book in his dad's study.

Shadow Dent leaned forward in his chair. It was hard to tell through frosted glass, but it seemed like he was reacting to something he didn't like.

"You're new here, right?" the secretary asked.

Please, miss. I know you're trying to be nice, but I really want to know my fate before I walk through that door. I beg of you, let me listen in peace. Or whatever it's called when there is quiet, and you're trying to listen in on a conversation that's not meant for you to hear. "Yes, ma'am," he said instead. "We moved here from Texas over Christmas break."

Wait. Is that music coming from the principal's office?

Shadow Dent stood up. The principal said something sharp, and Dent dropped back in his chair like a bag of farmer's-market-sourced apples.

"I'll be honest, the rain takes some getting used to, but you'll like the summers more," the secretary said.

Oh my god, lady! Please, please. Just let me sit here. Please, I'm begging you. "Yeah, for sure," Geoff said. "In Texas, it feels like the sun wants to punish you for being outside." *Geoff, why are you making conversation?*

"I think you'll find the sun here quite welcoming once it finally arrives. I'm Ms. Gilroy, by the way," the secretary said. "But everyone just calls me Janet."

"I don't think I'm allowed to call teachers by their first name."

"It's OK, I'm not a teacher, and Janet isn't my first name," Janet said. "It's Michelle."

Suddenly, Geoff was less interested in what was happening in the principal's office. "I'm sorry, what?"

"Yeah, apparently people think I look like—"

The principal's door flew open, and a red-faced Dent appeared. "GILM!," he said.

Is he talking to me?

"GILM!," Janet replied. Her demeanor had shifted. She took off her glasses and met Dent with a stare that burned like a Texas summer sun.

"GILM!," said a voice from the office. Geoff recognized the principal's voice from morning announcements and school assemblies. Whatever that "GILM!" meant, she didn't like Dent's "GILM!" either.

"GILM!," Dent responded. "I saw him GILM! and I responded as required."

"GILM!," the principal replied.

"GILM!!" exclaimed Mr. Dent.

The three of them went round and round until their "GILM!"s converged. Soon, their heated argument settled into a soothing mantra of "GILM!"s.

Watching the intensity of Janet and Mr. Dent's expressions fade to half-lidded masks was an unsettling sight to behold.

That seems bad. Are things getting worse? I think things are getting worse. I wonder if I can just leave.

Geoff gingerly curled his fingers around the strap of his backpack and stood slowly.

No reaction from the three authority figures.

He reversed out of the room like he was stepping through a minefield and quickened his pace as he cleared the doorway.

That book is toast.

Wait, no. It's ash.

Whatever, I'm burning it.

The Mangled
Middle Eight

"You're home early," Geoff's dad said.

Why was his dad home? Did the principal call him? Geoff let his bag slide to the kitchen floor as he used his foot to shut the back door behind him.

Why does he look like that? Why would a man who described himself as a "natty dresser" wear a wrinkled shirt with his sleeves rolled up over his elbows? And why did his hair look like he'd been pulling at its ends all morning?

Also, why was he sitting at the kitchen table facing the back door?

Because he wants to kill me with disappointed eyes. I'm going to implode due to my father's disappointment.

"Have a seat," his dad said.

In Geoff's experience, there was never a positive conversation with the offer of a seat. Like, *Have a seat. Good news, you've won the lottery.* Or *Have a seat, here's a puppy.* It was always *Have a seat, I heard what you did at school today,* or *Have a seat, we're moving,* or *Have a seat, buddy, I saw your browser history. You know, when a man and a woman love each other very much . . .*

That last one was definitely the worst and most awkward conversation of his life to date. Still, this next one might give it a run for its money. *So, you're skipping school . . .* Or worse, *So, you're unraveling society, son, let's talk about it.*

His dad remained silent until Geoff sat down and pulled his chair closer to the table. Geoff folded his hands in front of him and prepared for the worst.

"So, you found the book," his dad said.

"What book?"

"Nice try. GI—" His dad swallowed like he was trying to keep a bad egg salad sandwich down. He'd actually seen his dad do that before, and it literally looked the same. Only that time, his dad had immediately booked it to the bathroom. This time, however, he just sat and glared at him.

He'd never seen his dad glare before.

"OK, so I found the book," Geoff said.

"Why did you go through my GILM!—" His dad clenched his jaw and shook his head. "Why did you go through my things?"

"I didn't mean to. I just wanted to see it."

His dad's face was hard to read. He looked mad, not disappointed, which in this case felt just as bad as when he was disappointed somehow. *This man really has some range.*

But something else was happening with his father. Like he was trying to fight a case of hiccups. A really bad case of hiccups. A case of the hiccups fit for a write-up in *The New England Journal of Medicine.*

It was one thing when Geoff thought about how his dumb wish was affecting the world around him. That was impersonal. Just a bunch of students and teachers he didn't know well at all.

But this was his dad, and unlike everyone else at school, the professor knew exactly what was going on.

"There are very clear warnings at the beginning of each chapter."

Oh, so that's what that was. Maybe the person who wrote it should have put it in huge font in the middle of the page. Like, "Warning! This book is dangerous." And not in cursive so that people could read it in the future.

"I'm sorry," Geoff said.

"Is that why you're home early?"

"Yeah. I came home to burn the book."

His dad's eyebrows raised. "Burn the book? Why?"

"Because if the book ceases to exist, the spell can't exist."

"Son." His dad shook his head. "No."

"'No' what?"

"If I hadn't been here and you burned this book, we would have no way to try to reverse this spell. Where did you get in your head that burning it would make it go away?"

"I don't know," Geoff said. "It seemed like a good idea."

"OK." His dad's shoulders relaxed. "For the record, that was a bad plan."

"OK, geez," Geoff said.

"Sorry, just wanted to make it clear—very bad plan."

"Dad, I get it."

"Like, where would you have burned it? In the fireplace? Do you know what the magical blowback would do to this house?"

"Dad, OK, you've made your point."

"Speaking of points." He produced a long decorative hat pin and pricked his thumb before pressing it into the book's cover. "I suppose you didn't read this part, did you?"

Geoff shook his head.

"The book requires a blood sacrifice, although it doesn't say how much."

"What? You said not to give it blood!" Geoff exclaimed.

His dad looked confused. "What are you talking about?"

"Back at the store the other day. You said not to give it blood."

"That was a different thing! Geoff, how many times have I explicitly stated to read directions first?"

"I don't know," Geoff said. His dad did say that a lot. But unlike when the professor was growing up, people made things easy to understand now. Products had stickers that showed you how to start them, software that walked you through everything you needed to do, which was usually just to hit the next button and click a box saying you'd read the terms of service, which, of course, you hadn't. Who had time for that?

His dad shook his head. "From everything I've gathered, this should be enough to find the answers we're
looking for." His father scanned the table of contents
and asked if Geoff had read the incantation from chapter 12.

*Why are there so many chapters on wishing in
that book? Wait, why am I focused on the amount of
chapters when dad just said something about a blood
sacrifice? Also, is that why he has so many hat pins?*

His dad used a non-bloody finger to skim a page. He
flipped to the next page and then the next before going
back to the page before. "Did the volume of your voice
increase unnaturally when you read the incantation?"

"I don't think so," Geoff said.

"OK. Are your GILM!— Blast!" His dad shook
his head like a dog shaking out its coat. "Are your ears
ringing right now?"

"No," Geoff said.

His dad flipped back to the table of contents and
scanned until he found another option, then thumbed
through to the chapter. He peered at the ceiling and
tapped a forefinger to his lips. "Did your eyes sting
afterward?"

Geoff shook his head.

His dad returned to the table of contents and then to
a new chapter.

"Did your arm hair grow significantly before reced-
ing to normal?"

"I don't know," Geoff said. "Would I have
noticed?"

His dad cocked an eyebrow. "You would have noticed," he said, and dove back to the table of contents. "Did an upside-down talking cat head appear and ask you a riddle?"

"Definite no there, Dad. I probably would have come to you on that."

"Good man." His dad went back to the table of contents, checking and double-checking the chapter. "OK, I think this is GILM!." He pulled at his collar. "I think this is it. Did the words you read aloud sound like gibberish to your ears?"

Geoff's eyes sparked to life like an old misfiring lighter that finally struck a flame. "Yes!"

His dad pumped a fist like he was bringing an invisible hatchet to rest on the table. He scanned the page with an index finger. "Hmm," he said, then reread the paragraph. He covered his eyes with the palms of his hands and leaned back into his chair.

"What?" Geoff asked.

"Well, I GILM!— I found the cure, but I don't GILM!—" He shook his head. "It's getting worse," he said, blinking like he was trying to get something out of his eyes.

"You OK?" Geoff asked.

"I'll be fine," his dad replied. "Probably. Anyway, not important. Here's the thing." His father cleared his throat. "You need to supply the book with the blood of your enemy and say the incantation again, backward. Listen to me, GILM!— Listen to me, Geoff."

His dad leaned forward.

Here we go. The ol' "but you can't take the blood of another person" trope. There has to be another way, blah blah blah.

"You have to mean it, son. You have to really want to reverse this."

I'm sorry, what? He actually wants me to take someone else's blood and feed it to this book?

"Dad, how am I supposed to take someone's blood?"

"Not just someone, GILM!— Not just someone. Your enemy. Do you have an enemy?"

It didn't take a lot of thought. "Yeah, this guy named Will. I see him every day at the bike racks."

"That's good, son."

"Is it? Dad, why does it require the blood of my enemy this time? That doesn't make any sense."

"Because the natural opposing desire from your enemy counteracts the initial will behind the wish."

"Initial Will. Geez, Dad, you make puns even when you don't mean to. I guess that makes sense."

His dad checked his watch and then exhaled a frustrated breath.

"What?"

"It's almost five o'clock. Your school has been out for a while."

"No big deal, Dad, I'll see him tomorrow morning. Believe me, the hard part will be getting his blood."

"That's not so hard," his dad said.

The way he said it caught Geoff off guard. The warm, thoughtful man that Geoff had known his entire life had just brushed off the acquisition of someone's blood like it was ordering takeout. "We GILM!—don't GILM!—don't have until tomorrow."

"How much time do we have?"

His dad shrugged his shoulders. "Midnight, maybe? GILM! . . . but probably nine o'clock."

"Nine o' clock?" Geoff asked. "What kind of spell cements or lifts at nine o'clock? I've never heard of that before."

"It's midnight GILM!— Eastern time. These spells were created in New England."

"Spells revert to time zones? Wouldn't they correspond to, like, the phase of the moon or something?"

His dad squinted up at the ceiling. "You know, I think everyone on Earth sees the same moon phase at the same time, but that's not all really important. What is important is that the group that curated this book was trying to redraw the world with their town as the central hub—"

"Central hub? I thought you said eastern," Geoff joked.

His dad looked confused, then allowed himself a grin. "I'm the GILM!" The professor coughed into his fist. "Hey, I'm the dad, so I'm the one who makes time-zone puns here, son. Anyway, I think the spell is tethered to the location. Also, we need to take into account that clocks weren't exactly precision instruments at the time of this writing."

"OK, so it really could be anytime?"

"Don't worry about that."

"OK," Geoff said, and leaned back into his chair.

His dad's eyes narrowed. "Worry about it a little bit."

Geoff leaned forward.

"Now, where can we find your enemy?"

Was Will the type of guy who would show up unannounced at his sister's date to embarrass the kid he was bullying?

Without a doubt.

"I have a date at six."

"You have a date." His dad pinched the bridge of his nose. "Son, while I'm happy for you, I need you to stay focused—"

"Don't worry, Dad," Geoff said. "He'll find me."

"OK." His dad reached down below the table and rummaged around in his old satchel for a few seconds before he brought out a leather bundle. He rolled out what looked like a chef's knife bag or something out of a Dracula movie montage where Van Helsing puts together his crew. Geoff's eyes bugged as he zeroed in on a literal sharpened stake.

Who was his father?

"Now, you want something that will cut with a glancing strike," his dad said while examining the edge of a small hatchet.

"Dad, how am I supposed to inconspicuously carry a freaking axe around?"

"Why do you need to be inconspicuous?"

"Because I'm going on a date."

"GILM! . . . that's right. Your date." His father

tucked the hatchet back into the leather roll and cocked his head toward his son. "What's her— GILM!." His dad's hands gripped the side of the table. "What's her name?"

"Corinne."

"Nice name, son. That's a nice GILM!— That's a nice name."

"Her brother, Will, is the guy who bullies me at school."

Dimples creased his dad's face on either side of a pleasant grin. "So, is it a date or a trap?"

"Yes," Geoff said.

His dad rubbed his eyes and quietly laughed. "Alright, get showered up. Take your pocketknife and GILM!— And this." His dad pulled a syringe from the leather roll.

"You want me to drug him?"

His dad gazed toward the ceiling, then refocused his eyes on Geoff. "You know, I didn't think about that, but GILM!— But I don't have what I'd need for it here. Just ask him for some blood."

"Just casually ask for some blood."

"Or you can take it."

The Darker Notes

Geoff jumped in the shower without waiting for the water to warm up. Corinne would be at his front door soon, and he had no time to spare.

He couldn't stop replaying how casually his dad had told him to take someone's blood. Sure, this seemed like an end-of-the-world event, but it was still weird.

How was he going to draw blood from Will? Would the guy pop up in the window of the pizza place like an overly aggressive piece of toast, or would he just pull up a chair—

Ah!

Geoff had forgotten to turn on the cold with the hot. He'd missed the whole tuning-of-the-water-temp bit by just hopping in. Maybe that's what you get when you don't have a plan.

Geoff toweled off and got ready for his date. He threw on his best pair of jeans, which he kept at the back of his drawer for special occasions, and buttoned up his favorite flannel with the least wrinkles. He put his hand over the pocketknife and syringe he'd set on his dresser but decided to put his shoes on first before sticking them in his pocket.

Am I procrastinating or just determining a work-flow? Hmm, workflow, definitely workflow.

He turned his attention to the macabre task that awaited him. How was he going to initiate the bloodletting that the book required?

Maybe I'll just ask Will to go outside.

And then what? It's cold out there, so the only thing exposed will be his hands and face. I am not slashing anyone's face, so I guess his hand.

Maybe he could just ask for some blood. But why would Will do that? What if Geoff offered to never see Corinne again? That could work, especially if the date wasn't going well.

Even if it was, he could just lie. What was the harm in lying to save the world, after all? Besides, lying was way better than stabbing—

What was that?

A knock.

Geoff checked his watch. Corinne was early. He eyed the pocketknife and syringe. *I'll get them in a second.*

He scrambled to lace up his boots. He'd never been a lace-up-boot guy before Portland, but living in a world full of puddles with unidentified depths really makes a guy rethink his footwear. He stopped to check his hair in the mirror. It looked pretty good except for one strand that kept flying up. He tried pressing it down, but no luck.

He tried tucking it in under other hair, which only worked for a second.

Knock knock knock.

He licked his hand and tried to stick it down, running his hand through his hair again and again. Finally, it stayed down. But something else caught his eye.

He'd misbuttoned his shirt.

He quickly unbuttoned and rebuttoned and returned his gaze to the mirror. Now he had two flyaway hairs hovering on either side of his head like alien antennae.

Knock knock knock.

Why wasn't his dad answering the door?

Geoff slid his weathered jacket on and held his hands over his hair as he tromped down the half-spiral stairway and approached the front door. He saw her before she saw him. She looked beautiful. The natural look from school was subtly accented by eyeliner and lipstick, and her hair was pulled away from her face by two tiny braids that connected behind her head.

And she looked nervous.

What does she have to be nervous about?

Her eyes curved into little rounded hills as she noticed Geoff's approach through the glass and wood-latticed front door.

"Dad?" Geoff called.

"Have GILM!— Have fun, but remember GILM! . . . nine o' clock," his dad responded from the bathroom. His voice sounded strained, which wasn't unusual for a voice coming from the bathroom, but something told Geoff there was more to it.

Geoff had a plan and a date. He'd either accomplish his mission or have one last moment of happiness before the world spun into chaos.

"Greetings, Earthling," Corinne said as Geoff opened the door.

"Huh?"

"Your hair," she said. "You have some flyaways."

Geoff checked his reflection in the window. *Oh my god, this is humiliating.*

"Don't worry, I got you," Corinne said while digging through an oversized black canvas bag. She pulled out a small circular container and put some goop on her hand before tossing it back into the bag. She rubbed her hands together like a doctor about to check a lymph node. "Here, let's try this."

She ran her hands through his hair, scrunching and curling her fingers as she went. Their eyes met as she pulled away.

There was something about meeting someone's eyes like that. Geoff had never dared to maintain that type of eye contact before, but now he couldn't look away. His heart felt like a power plant that pumped electricity through his veins and to every single nerve ending along his arms.

"That's better," she said. She straightened his collar and rubbed her fingers along the fabric.

"Oh," Geoff said. "Was my collar messed up?"

"Not really. I just wanted to wipe the pomade off without you noticing."

"You know, we have a sink. Not to brag, but two, actually. You can wash your hands."

"I don't want to be late," she said. "You look great, by the way, even as an alien."

You idiot, Geoff. You're supposed to compliment her.

She had one side of her hair in a braid while the other flowed naturally. Geoff didn't know much about women's hair care, but it was a pretty safe bet she'd spent some time on it.

"You look amazing, I like your hair like that. The braid thing."

She smiled and looked away for a moment before returning her gaze. "Kind of sounds like something an alien would say. You sure you're not an alien? You have to tell me if you are, it's the law."

"I come in peace," Geoff said.

She grabbed his sleeve. "Let's go, I want to get a booth."

Corinne gently led the way down the stairs toward a light blue five-door Subaru. The lights blinked as she made her way around to the driver's-side door.

A car started up down the block, and headlights sprang to life as Geoff touched the handle of the passenger-side door.

It would be funny if that's Will.

OK, not funny, but a coincidence, maybe? But if he has a car, why would he always be at the bike racks?

The Crescendo
of Chaos

Apizza Disaction had a line out the door with people chunked in groups. Some chatted about pizza toppings, some about vintage arcade games, and one guy was in the middle of a hard sell to his friends. "Yeah, there's this article that claimed this place has the best pizza in the country. The internet went crazy saying it was impossible for Portland to have the best pizza, but for real, this place is so good."

Geoff slowed his pace as they approached the back of the line against the blue-green walls of the apparently nationally acclaimed pizza joint, but Corinne just grinned at him like he was a toddler trying to pronounce "spaghetti." She gently grasped his hand and squeezed them past a group of people who, judging by their annoyed faces, had been waiting in the queue for quite some time.

Once they were inside, a woman in a ringer tee stepped toward them, all smiles and braids. She nodded the pair toward an open booth with a grip of menus in her hand.

The people along the bar ate pizza from elevated platters and drank craft brews under the eighties-style logo for the restaurant. Booths lined the walls, with four-top tables sprinkled in between. There was even a game room off to the side with the old stand-up arcade games from back in the day.

Geoff did his best to conceal how much he enjoyed their skip-the-line VIP treatment as they made their way to the booth. He didn't want Corinne to see him as some wide-eyed new kid, so he decided to mask his excitement with aloofness.

Or at least his best approximation. Geoff hadn't been aloof for one day of his life and was hyperaware of that fact.

His face kept checking in with his brain to see if they held their mouth right. *Should our lips be down? The aloof don't smile, right?*

No, it's not a frown, face. It's more like a null expression.

Null? Brain, when did we start using words like "null"? Like, I know what it means, it's just weird that we chose this exact moment to use it.

Hey, what are the eyebrows doing right now? Why are they up so high? You're making us look like an idiot.

They slid into the booth, and Geoff stared out the window. One, because he thought it looked aloof to stare off into space, and two, because he wanted to catch his reflection to see what his face was doing and if his flyaway hair strands had managed to stay in place during the quick trip from his house to the pizza joint.

"So, how do you like it here?" Corinne asked.

Just calmly turn your attention away from the window, Geoff. Let her see it's no big deal for you to talk to a girl. And not just any girl, the one girl you've been crushing on since your first day of school.

Corinne neatly folded her hands in front of her and leaned slightly forward.

Ah, now look at her. That's better than aloof, Geoff. See? She's relaxed. Relaxed! That's what we should be. Look how confident she is. God, I would give anything to be that confident.

Take it easy, Geoff, we're already dealing with the fallout from one of your wishes, don't wish for more.

Oh my god, just answer her question. Do you like Portland? Yes, the answer is yes. She is from here, so you should answer yes.

"Uh," Geoff said.

Oh wow, good start, buddy.

"I like it okay. I never thought I'd wear sweaters and hoodies this much. You know, in Texas, the winter is freezing in the morning and then seventy-five degrees when you get out of school, so it's really hard to plan what to wear. Also, everything here is bike friendly. In Houston, there aren't really any bike lanes, so it was mostly either the school bus or hitching a ride in a friend's car."

"I meant here. This place." She tapped on the table. "What do you think?"

Oh my god, this specific place, of course. Nice rambling new-kid exposition, bud.

Should I act like we have better stuff in Houston right now, or should I admit this is the best pizza place I've ever been to? Even before I've tasted a slice of pizza, I know it beats all the cookie-cutter chain places from back home.

Dude, you've already insulted her musical, just say it's great.

"Oh, yeah, Apizza Disaction. It's great. I love the whole vintage vibe."

Corinne's grazel eyes sparkled. "This is my dad's place. He started here as a driver before he met my mom and worked his way up."

"For real? That's amazing."

"Yeah, the name comes from the old guy that ran the place before him. He was looking to retire and asked my dad if he wanted a piece of the action."

Geoff replayed what she had just said in his head several times. "Apizza Disaction . . . a piece of this action. Oh my god, your dad is worse than my dad. That's next-level punning."

"Dad jokes are the best slash worst," Corinne said. She was fully leaning forward now. "What does your dad do?"

You know those kids who dress in all black and sit on the floor in the corner of the cafeteria every day for some reason instead of using the tables like everyone else? He's their king.

Nah, don't say that, Geoff. You'll sound like a jerk. Just say he's a teacher and get on with it. She doesn't need to know about his weird store.

"My dad's a professor over at Reese."

"Oh? What does he profess?" Corinne leaned back and kicked a knee up on the edge of the booth as she basked in her terrible pun.

"Please, no, not you, too," Geoff said. "They have you. The dads have you. You're becoming one of them!"

"Like the body snatchers movie?" Corinne's eyes went dull, and she held her hands out like a zombie. "One of us, one of us."

"Haha, yeah, exactly," Geoff replied. But what she'd just said gave him pause.

That's kind of what's happening when someone says "GILM!" . . .

Geoff's mind snapped back to his side quest for the night. Maybe it should have been the main mission, but it was hard to tell when he was sitting across from the crush of his life on a date that was already going way better than he could have imagined. And he had a pretty good imagination.

"Can I get you started with something to drink?" The woman in braids was back.

Corinne slid the foot she had propped up on the edge of the seat under the table. "This is Geoff." She motioned to him and then back to the woman in braids. "Geoff, this is my sister, Sally."

My Sister Sally would be a great name for a band, Geoff thought. "Nice to meet you, Sally."

Sally curled a handful of menus behind her and leaned against the table. "So, you're the 'GILM!' guy."

"He's the 'GILM!' guy," Corinne affirmed.

"I'm the 'GILM!' guy," Geoff said. He thought he'd complete the triad. He'd recently seen something about the rule of three in comedy in a video. But something shifted in the rule of three as a murmuring of "GILM!"s rumbled through the restaurant.

Geoff tried not to squirm in his seat. *Well, at least they're not chanting.*

"Love your song," Sally said.

"Thanks," Geoff replied. He wondered if he was blushing, so he quickly glanced at the window to check his reflection again for flyaways. Sally had such a kind face between those braids. A face you'd see on a billboard ad to welcome you to a town, a pizza place, or a family. The polar opposite of the face that stared daggers on the other side of the window. Will's face.

Daggers.

Geoff's hand instinctively shot to his jacket pocket to check for his pocketknife. *Did I forget to put it in there before going downstairs?* He checked the other, but both pockets were empty. *Please, please, past-Geoff, please have decided to put them in your jeans instead.* He felt his right pant pocket but just felt the outline of his phone. His other hand clapped over the other pocket, only to feel his keys.

He'd left his knife and the syringe on the dresser at home. *Oh my god, all I had to do was drop them into my jacket pocket, but no, I had to be Mr. Lace-up-your-boots-first Guy for some reason. Great, Geoff, just great.*

"I think he's embarrassed by the attention," Corinne said.

Geoff did his best not to look like a nervous wreck. "Yeah, it's really nice of you to say. I'm glad you like it."

"It's GILM!," Sally replied.

Once again, a low murmuring of "GILM!"s spread across the kitschy little pizza joint.

"Corinne was so excited this afternoon. I helped her with her hair, and Mom had to practically pry her away from the mirror—"

"Thank you, Sally!" Corinne interrupted. Her eyes widened, then narrowed as her jaw slid forward. "You-can-go-get-the-drinks-now, bye!"

Sally grinned. "Have fun, you two."

Corinne leaned back against the booth. "So embarrassing."

"I don't know," Geoff said. "I think it's great you're close with your family."

He'd often wondered what it would be like to have a family like that. Both a mom and a dad, maybe a brother or sister or two. In his imaginings, they all got along, played the same games, liked the same shows, and cracked each other up at the dinner table each night. He knew that wasn't how real families behaved, but it was something to think about when he was sitting alone in his room.

"Hi, Will," Corinne said. Her eyes focused just above Geoff's right shoulder.

Will.

"Hello, Dirt," Will said.

"I think you mispronounced 'Corinne,'" Geoff said. "The C is more of a K sound, like 'knife.'"

Corinne tried to hold back a laugh, but it escaped like an excited terrier squeezing through your legs when you open the door to accept a package.

Will, much like the delivery guy, did not look amused. "But then, wouldn't it sound like Orinne?"

"So, not Dirt, then?"

"Look," Will said. "Can I talk to you outside?"

Geoff sat still for a moment and marveled that his plan had almost gone to perfection. Not only had he kept his date with Corinne, but Will had shown up just like a monster in the basement at the end of a horror movie.

And much like in a horror movie, Geoff found himself utterly unprepared for the situation. Although he'd thought through everything up and to the moment, he'd forgotten the implements to his success: a pocketknife and a syringe.

"Yeah, maybe later, Will?" Geoff replied.

"You two know each other," Corinne said.

Usually people ask something like that as a question. *You two know each other?* A story trope as old as time immemorial, but Corinne had just said it flatly.

Will gripped his hands into fists that hovered beside him.

Why is Will the only guy here in short sleeves? It's like forty-six degrees outside.

"GILM!?" Will asked, or said. It sounded like a question, but Geoff wasn't a hundred percent certain.

"GILM!" repeated around the room in a whisper. Not a rumble, not a murmur, but in unison. Trailing away like a passing car.

"Will, Sally was looking for you," Corinne said.

"Nice try, Dirt."

"Will!" Sally called from behind the bar.

The muscles in Will's jaw clenched as he shook his head. "Coming," he said through gritted teeth. It seemed to take a lot of effort to tear his attention away from Geoff.

Will slid by a server who arrived with their drinks, napkins, and cutlery.

Geoff eyed the black handle of what looked like a steak knife sticking out of the top of a red plastic cup. Maybe that would do the trick later when, ultimately, Will dragged him outside to beat the life out of him.

"I'm sorry about my brother," Corinne said as she arranged the plates and set the flatware beside them. "He can be a lot."

"Yeah," Geoff said quietly.

Now that the danger had passed, he noticed that his shoulders were curved in toward each other, his arms together, and his hands fitted prayer style between his knees. How he could be so different from one moment to the next? How could part of him believe that he could do something as great as writing the perfect song or touring the country, when another part of him couldn't stop criticizing himself?

"Why is Will like that?" Geoff asked.

Corinne's fingers intertwined in front of her, and she stared into her palms as though she'd find the answer written there in some sort of mystical ink.

Geoff wondered what the backstory could be for the Will he saw every day at the bike rack and what Corinne saw at home. Maybe Will was overcompensating for some traumatic childhood event. Maybe someone bullied him when he was a freshman, so he thought it was a rite of passage.

Maybe, in his own way, he was just a protective brother.

Corinne exhaled. "I don't know, to be honest. He's just kind of always been a dick."

"Well, alright," Geoff said, leaning back and blinking. *Then I guess he has this coming to him.* He set his hand over the serrated pizza knife and palmed it.

"What's that?" Geoff asked, and pointed off into the distance.

"What's what?" Corinne replied.

Geoff slid the knife down below the table, out of Corinne's eye line, and into the pocket of his jacket. *Wait, will the blood stay on the knife blade? I just want a glancing cut, not a stab wound. Like, stabbing is a crime-crime. A slice to save the world is more like mischief.*

"That game. Do you know what that game is called?"

"Uh, Donkey Kong?" Corinne asked. Her eyebrows raised in disbelief. "You've never seen a Donkey Kong machine before?"

Of course I've seen Donkey Kong. And it's so much fun to say. Donkey Kong, Donkey Kong, Donkey Kong. Why'd I have to point at that one? Oh well, just shrug. It's not lying if it's a shrug, right?

Corinne leaned in. "Oh my god, I can't wait to show you—"

"Here's your pizza," Will said. The metal tray that held the pie clattered onto the table. It was loud enough to draw the attention of most of the room, but Will didn't seem to care. "Ge-off, you want to step outside for a quick GILM!?"

"GILM!"s reverberated around the room.

"Not really," Geoff said. "We just got our pizza."

"Will, leave," Corrinne said.

"Will!" Sally called from the back.

Will glared at Geoff.

"Will!" Sally repeated.

Will growled before ripping his glare away like the end of a receipt from the machine at the pizza counter. "Fine, I'm coming." He glanced back one more time before skulking off toward the bar or whatever lair he'd carved out in the ground below.

"I'm so sorry," Corinne said.

"Don't be. It's not like you're doing it."

"Still, the guy is such a GILM!"

Whispered "GILM!"s were chanted across the room like a wave rolling over Apizza Disaction. Geoff knew it was getting worse. Corinne's "GILM!"s weren't as bad as his father's yet, but his dad had a head start hearing the song.

Geoff checked his watch. It was seven thirty, which meant there was plenty of time to eat, get some blood, and drive back home for a little reverse-o spell action.

Something on the table caught his attention. Something green. *Why is there green on the pizza?*

"Hey, Corinne, what is . . . this?"

The pizza had lettuce-y leaves with strips of what looked like translucent bacon, white crumbles of cheese, and something drizzled over the top of it all.

"Prosciutto, arugula, feta, and a honey drizzle," Corinne said. "It's my favorite. Come on, we talked about this."

Oh, that's right, she warned me. This is so weird, it looks like a salad with a crust. "It looks delicious," Geoff said.

Corinne took a slice from the tray and put it on her plate. "Go on, try it. You'll love it."

I bet you're wrong.

Geoff did his best to smile and look hungry as he slid a slice onto his plate. He rotated it and realized it might be the last thing he ate before the end of the world as he knew it. Or was it the end of language? Whatever was about to happen if he didn't get some of the blood of his enemy home and into that old thirsty book.

"You're scared," Corinne said. "Don't be scared of pizza."

"I'm not scared. I'm just . . . marveling."

"You're marveling?"

"What? I can marvel. It's a word."

"Well, marvel that into your mouth, big guy. Time to bring some new GILM! into your life."

Another wave of "GILM!"s rolled over the pizza place.

Just do it, man. You don't have much more time.

Geoff brought the slice to his mouth and kept his lips as far away from the honey drizzle as physically possible. He wasn't a big fan of honey and certainly couldn't understand why someone would ruin a perfectly good pizza by drizzling it on top. But then again, they'd already ruined it by putting a freaking salad on top of it instead of pepperoni.

Maybe if I just swallow it down quickly I won't taste it.

Geoff bit down and realized it wasn't something he was going to be able to swallow without chewing first. And a good, solid chew, at that.

What even is arugula?

Corinne's eyebrows raised as she leaned forward. Geoff wondered for a moment if it was all a prank.

Wait, this is delicious. What the heck? Arugula is like spicy lettuce.

Corinne grinned. "See?"

Geoff nodded as he swallowed down the first bite. "You're right. This is great."

"GILM!"

Another wave of whispered "GILM!"s passed through Apizza Disaction, but this time, the wave rolled back.

Geoff shifted in his seat and checked in with himself. Was his imagination catastrophizing the situation with all the "GILM!"s? He looked at a four-top deep in conversation. Pleasantly locked in on one another. That is, until someone said "GILM!."

It probably wasn't catastrophizing if it was in the middle of an actual catastrophe. He had to do something. And the something he had to do was not going to be pleasant.

He took another couple of bites as though the secret to calming his nerves was more pizza. Although, in his experience, more pizza certainly wouldn't hurt the situation.

Except that one time at Maria Lopez's birthday party in seventh grade where he ate way more pizza than he should have before everyone went out to jump on the trampoline.

Think about something else—anything but that stupid trampoline party. Let's see, Muppets, the news, carrots, or music. Music, yeah, that's it. Wait, what are they playing over the speakers right now?

The blood seemed to freeze in Geoff's arms.

Oh no. They're playing it over the speakers. This is bad.

How could a stupid wish to impress a girl turn into a world event? Would it be a world event, or just regional? How was the magic supposed to work?

"GILM!" Will said. His face was as red as the pepperoni on the pizza that Geoff would have typically ordered. Once again his hands were clenched into fists at his sides, and he motioned with his head toward the door.

"Will, go away," Corinne said. "GILM!"

Geoff wasn't sure if that was a substitute for a curse word or a curse word unto itself, but whatever it was, she meant it.

Will didn't take his eyes off Geoff, and this time Sally was in the weeds behind the bar. The place was packed, so there was no calling him back.

Geoff checked his watch. It was closing in on eight o'clock. If he was going to get some blood, he might as well do it now. He was running out of time.

"Fine," Geoff said. He wiped his mouth and folded his napkin before laying it on the table. "This will just take a second, Corinne."

"Geoff, don't."

"It'll be fine," Geoff said. "We're just going to talk."

"GILM!" Will reiterated.

"OK," Geoff said. "Maybe it won't be just a talk, but I'm a terrible fighter, so it won't take long."

The Resonant Tone
of Repercussions

Geoff had barely turned the corner outside Apizza Disaction before Will's fist met the bridge of his nose.

It took him a few moments to realize what had happened. There was a crunching sound, his world blinked white, and his ears rang. He'd never been hit in the face before, and already he'd have preferred not to repeat the experience.

"GILM!" Will said.

Geoff immediately understood that "GILM!" meant that Will wanted him to stay away from his sister. He had to admit the efficiency of using one word to convey so much information. Maybe the GILM! curse wouldn't be so bad after all?

"Now, wait just a second," Geoff said. "For real, hang on." He felt the bridge of his nose to see if it was still in the same place. "Just wait. That hurt. I need to get my bearings. My head is a little spinny."

Will's fist slammed into Geoff's gut, forcing him to double over. Geoff wasn't exactly sure what to do. He hadn't ever been in a fight before. Not really. A couple of shoving matches in junior high, but nothing that ever came to blows. How did people shrug punches off so easily in movies?

His stomach gurgled its own response, full of intention, which was to evict its present contents if that type of behavior kept up. It was about to be Maria Lopez's birthday party all over again. "Will, I think I might be sending the pizza back in your direction. It was delicious and all, but the service here is terrible. Two stars."

Geoff hunched over and stared at the ground. It was funny, the things he noticed while in a situation he'd rather not be in. The loose gravel in the parking lot, a stink bug trundling across the loose gravel, and Will's boot behind his ankle.

Now why would Will's boot be there—

Meaty hands pushed him backward, and Geoff went sprawling onto the pavement. Once he was down, he rolled to his side and propped himself up on an elbow. The pizza knife in his jacket pocket was calling to him, and he knew what he needed to do.

Or did he?

Although Will may have had a bloodletting coming, something wasn't clicking for Geoff. He knew what the plan to save the world required and the consequences of failure, but as he peered up at his bully, he wondered if he could really be someone who would use a knife on another human being.

No. No way. I can't just walk around like normal after stabbing someone. There's no coming back from something like that. Will may deserve a reckoning, but not that. Besides, I'm the one who invited this conflict. I knew what I was doing.

God, I'm such an idiot.

I wouldn't even be in this situation if I'd just acted like musicals were my thing. It's not even that hard of a stretch. Concerts are basically musicals these days with lights and video timed to music. But no, I had to be Mr. Contrarian. Why can't I ever stop myself from saying dumb things?

Geoff snapped his fingers. At least they would have snapped if they weren't so bloody, but he made the motion anyway since he had an idea.

That's it! It's me. I'm the enemy. I did this to myself. Now, do I have enough blood? Geoff gently pinched his nostrils and checked his fingers for blood. *Oh, yeah. Plenty of blood.*

"OK," Geoff said. "Let's call it a draw."

Will looked confused. Angry still, but confused.

"Will! Go home," Sally exclaimed. She must have noticed Will's absence and put two and two together. Fights were bad for business, and she did the thing where she screamed through her teeth like no one would notice that she was yelling and only her intended target would hear.

Geoff was pretty sure people were still staring. He and Will may have rounded the corner of the parking lot for privacy, but people usually come running as soon as they hear a fight.

"Will, you are such a dick!" Corinne scrambled toward Geoff as he stood up and wiped loose gravel out of the palms of his hands. Maybe she was the one to alert Sally, or maybe she'd been watching the whole time. Kind of hard to track that sort of thing when you're busy getting punched. "Are you OK?"

"Me?" Geoff asked. "I'm fine. Yeah, my face is all bloody, but you should see his knuckles. They're probably bloody too. And sure, faces are basically the main thing we use to identify other people, but you know, tomorrow morning, Will is going to, like, grip a fork or whatever . . . and the scabs will break, and it will sting. So, when you look at it like that, who really won the fight?"

"I think he has a concussion," Corinne said. "Maybe I should take him to the hospital."

"No!" Geoff composed himself. "I mean, no, thank you."

"Are you sure?" Corinne asked. "It's close."

"Do you think I could just get a ride back?" Geoff asked.

"GILM!?" Will said.

"Not you," Geoff replied.

The Haunting Harmony

The wipers on Corinne's car clicked a slow, metronomic beat as they slid across the windshield. Geoff flipped down the passenger-side visor and used its mirror to survey his face for damage. Even confronted with the world's end, he still wondered if there was a chance he and Corinne would kiss good night. He knew it was stupid, but he didn't care. That's the whole deal with crushes.

He inhaled deeply and exhaled slowly.

"You're different than I thought you'd be," Corinne said.

"Like bloodier, or . . ."

Corinne chuckled. "I mean, yeah, but, I don't know. You seem more confident than you do in class."

Geoff thought about it. *I guess she's right. I don't feel like I know anything or anyone in class. It's hard to project confidence in an environment like that. Hard for me, anyway.*

"Yeah, I don't know," Geoff said. "Maybe it's because I'm being asked questions about math."

"Geoff, we have history together."

"I guess that's why it's so weird that people ask me about math."

"Are you sure you don't have a concussion?"

"You can never be too sure. Are my pupils dilated?" Geoff leaned toward her with his eyes bugged out.

She palmed his face and playfully shoved it away. "GILM!," she said. Her hand shot to her mouth like she'd just uttered a terrible curse word or revealed something important. But unlike other "GILM!"s that Geoff had heard, that one felt different. Self-aware. The car slowed for a stop sign, and Corinne turned to Geoff. "That's not what I GILM!." Her jaw dropped, and her eyes darted to the side. "Why can't I say what I want to say?"

"What do you mean?" Geoff asked.

"Like I GILM!—" Her eyebrows narrowed, and her face flushed an angry red. "Like I'm trying to say something, but I'm interrupted by a 'GILM!.' What is happening, GILM!?"

How is she just now noticing? The only other person who seemed to have noticed is Dad.

Geoff checked the street sign as the car started moving again. They were only a couple of blocks away from his house. *I hope Dad has the anti-potion, or whatever we're calling it, all brewed up and ready to go.*

"You know that song I wrote?" he asked.

"GILM!"

"Yeah, that's right. Well, I kinda wished for it, and maybe that wish is a little bit cursed."

"A little bit cursed? GILM!!"

"And we kinda have to hurry back to my house if you don't want this to be permanent."

"GILM!?"

"Like we have until nine o'clock."

Corinne's eyes went wide as she pointed to the clock on the dashboard. It was eight fifty.

If I get through this, I really have to improve my time management skills.

Geoff shrugged and gave her his best and, hopefully, most adorable smile.

Corinne pressed down on the gas. "GILM!" She put her fist over her mouth like she was suppressing a burp and collected herself. "So, you went on a date while on a magical deadline?"

Wow, she just believes me. Really? Just immediate acceptance.

"I mean, it was kind of the whole point of the wish," Geoff said.

Corinne glared, glancing between him and the road. "That's sweet," she said.

"OK, that and I may have needed the blood of my enemy to break the spell."

"My brother's blood?" She pounded the steering wheel. "GILM!"

"Yeah, but I didn't do anything, remember? Well, I got hit, but that was more getting something done to me."

"GILM!"

"Corinne, I'm going to use my blood. I'm my own worst enemy."

"You used me."

Did I use her? I used the book to make a wish to impress her. Maybe I used her brother. No, I didn't even use him. I was going to but didn't. That should count for something, right?

"No. No, I didn't use you. Remember the wish? Wait, you believe the whole thing about the curse immediately, but not that I risked everything to go on a date with you?"

Corinne stared straight ahead and breathed out a slow breath. "GILM!"

The car slowed to a stop in front of his house, and Geoff turned in his seat. What did that "GILM!" mean? Acceptance? Disbelief? It didn't seem like anger, but it did seem sad.

Corinne pointed to her watch with big eyes and raised eyebrows. "GILM!"

"Oh! Yeah." Geoff understood that one and rushed to unbuckle his seat belt and pull the door's handle.

He bounded up the steps three at a time and fumbled in his pocket for his keys. Why didn't he have them ready to go? At this point, every second mattered. His dad's footsteps thumped solidly against the old wood floor of their craftsman house.

Geoff turned the key and put a shoulder to the door.

His dad stretched out his hands, his eyebrows raised high. "GILM!?"

"Yeah, I got the blood," Geoff said.

"GILM!," his father replied. He looked a little sweaty but relieved to see his son. He straightened the cuffs on his sleeves when he realized they had company. "GILM!," he said, offering his hand to Corinne, and she shook it.

"GILM!," she said.

"Did you get everything in the, um, cauldron?" Geoff asked.

"GILM!," his dad replied.

Geoff was pretty sure his dad meant yes, and they all hurried toward the kitchen. The clock on the microwave read 8:58.

"GILM!?" his dad asked. He wanted to make sure Geoff collected the blood of his enemy.

"Yeah," Geoff replied. "Not an un-ending supply, but plenty on-hand." Geoff ran his fingers along his nose like he was displaying a prize.

"GILM!," his dad said. Which meant *On-hand? More like on-face.*

Geoff rolled his eyes. Even facing a global catastrophe, his dad couldn't help but make dumb puns. "Good one, Dad."

His father grabbed him by the shoulders and stared into his soul. "GILM!?"

Geoff understood that his dad was asking him if he really believed in what he was about to do. Because he had to believe in the spell. He had to believe the blood would work and want everything to return to normal.

He believed the spell could work; that part was easy. He'd been living out its effects for the past day. He believed the blood would work because Will, on his worst day, couldn't make Geoff feel as small and insignificant as he made himself feel on almost a daily basis. Plus, it was completely his fault that he was in the whole situation to begin with.

So, did he really want everything to return to normal? These "GILM!"s were pretty effective at conveying complex messages with the efficiency of one syllable.

One syllable that, after one day, was already incredibly annoying.

"OK, how much blood does it need?" Geoff asked.

His dad shrugged and held up three fingers.

"Three what?"

"GILM!" His dad's fist shot to his mouth like he was suppressing a cough. His eyes sprang wide, and he twirled his hands in circles, indicating that Geoff should get going.

"OK, fine. Here goes." He squeezed his nose to get the blood flowing again. "Ow!"

He wondered if Corinne thought it was attractive in any way, shape, or form to see him this determined or if she just thought it was gross that he was basically playing with his own nose blood. Probably less gross than playing with someone else's nose blood, and certainly less sinister.

"GILM!," his dad said. He slammed the book down on the kitchen counter and jabbed a finger at the cover.

Geoff took a bloody thumb and pressed it in the same spot he'd seen his dad touch after the whole hat pin situation.

His dad opened the book, thumbed to the chapter, and pointed to a paragraph. "GILM!!"

Geoff squinted down at the page.

Add three drops of your enemy's blood, then repeat the incantation backward.

Geoff's eyes darted to the microwave clock. Eight fifty-nine. *How am I going to repeat this backward?*

"Do I just drop this on the page?"

"GILM!," his dad said.

That was a definite yes from his dad.

He held out his fingers and let a drop fall.

You always forget how red blood is until you see it right in front of you. Geoff was fascinated by how brilliant it looked against the tea-colored page, and just as interested in how quickly it disappeared.

"What the—GILM!?" Corinne's hands covered her mouth. She slowly lowered them as her eyes grew wider. "Is the book eating it? The book just ate your blood."

Geoff nodded. It was a strange feeling to be fascinated by magic in the midst of a magical catastrophe, but Geoff couldn't help but wonder what was going on with the book. Was it sentient? Did it need blood as food? Or was it some sort of mystical point-of-sale machine?

And if so, who or what was on the other side?

Geoff decided to put those thoughts away for the moment and went back to his nose for more blood, careful not to collect so much that he let four drops go instead of three. No telling what the spell would do with too much blood.

He held his hand over the book for another drop and eyed the clock. *Still eight fifty-nine, good.* He let his blood drop one last time.

"*GILM!,*" his father cried, and pointed to the page. "*GILM!!*"

"Yeah, I know!" Geoff said.

He obviously knew what to do, and now his dad was embarrassing him in front of Corinne, but Geoff didn't have time to worry about his pride. He needed to focus on the words. Maybe he should have done a vocal warm-up in the car. Corinne probably would have understood the pregame ritual with the whole musical background. What method would he have used? "Red leather, yellow leather"? "Rubber baby buggy bumpers"? How many tongue twisters were out there?

It wasn't important.

He exhaled and focused back on the page. His eyes wandered over to another paragraph on the left-hand side of the open book.

. . . incantation will nullify all results of previous effort. Any cost or benefit will be washed away. New relationships forgotten, progress lost, et cetera . . .

So, Corinne won't remember this at all? I'll just go back to being the weird, unconfident guy who sits next to her in class? The guy who insulted her musical?

"*GILM!!*" his dad exclaimed, and pointed to the clock on the microwave. "*GILM!!*"

It read nine o'clock.

The Stirring Solo

The clock on the microwave was fast. Geoff had set it a little earlier than the one on the oven to mess with his time-obsessed yet technically deficient father.

OK, remember you have to want this, Geoff. Wish to unwish the wish from yesterday. Got it? This is an unwish, no tricks. The book gets its blood, and I lose the girl, so it's kind of a double win for the book. I guess. Does the book care if I lose? Maybe I'm being presumptuous. Dang it, Geoff, focus. OK, I'm unwishing now. Here we go . . .

He began to read the incantation aloud, one word at a time, in reverse from the bottom of the paragraph. Slowly, the world faded away like someone had placed noise-canceling headphones around his ears.

Geoff could still hear the sounds from the incantation coming from him, but not the words. Amid the buzzy silence of the noise-canceling-headphones world, the vibration of the words rattled in his throat as he read them aloud, and just like the time before, they sounded like gibberish.

It was as though the incantation were a fishing line, and the magic was an enormous fish dragging the words out of him and back into the sea. His world pitched and tumbled like a ship in a storm.

He gripped the counter to keep his balance. He couldn't let the mystical waves throw him overboard in his own kitchen. Were his dad and Corinne experiencing the same shift? There was no time to check, and he had to maintain his focus. The whole world was relying on him.

He struggled to keep his eyes on the page of the old book as the words rushed out of him.

Geoff was pretty sure there weren't rapids in the ocean, but it started to feel that way. Like the whole kitchen was hurtling forward through space and time. The words came out of him faster, and it became more difficult to maintain his focus on the page.

The margins of his vision began to darken. The shadows crept closer, tighter and tighter, obstructing his field of view. It was getting harder to decipher the words on the page, like trying to read underwater.

The gibberish of the incantation and buzzy noise-canceling-headphone feeling merged together like an orchestra hurtling to a crescendo.

The lights blinked, and the shadows finally overwhelmed his field of vision. All he could see was darkness.

The room was quiet. Calm. At least Geoff hoped it was calm.

Did I finish? Am I alive?

Geoff wasn't sure if the curse had broken the proverbial fishing line and escaped out to sea, or if it was resting like an enormous shark skulking below a boat, just waiting for someone to dip a toe into the water.

"Dad?" Geoff blinked a couple of times until he could see the faint outlines of shapes in the darkness. *There's the skillet. OK, there's the stove. Good, I'm not blind.*

The lights blinked a couple of times before returning, and Geoff's eyes connected with his dad's in the reflection of the microwave door, each seeking hope in the other.

They were living in a moment between worlds. One where the spell had worked and everything was back to normal, and one where the world had unraveled into one-worded chaos.

His dad cleared his throat and rubbed his hands together. "Did it work?"

It worked. Oh, thank god, it worked.

His dad spun around like he'd just outbid some rando on eBay for a taxidermied raven once owned by Vincent Price or something. "It worked!"

Geoff wasn't sure if he felt relief or despair. Sure, they'd stopped the world from devolving into a one-word monoculture, but now he would have to start from scratch with Corinne. No, worse than scratch. Now she'd just remember him as the jerk who insulted her in class and then failed to come through with a song of his own.

How would anyone remember the past day? Like, would everyone just forget it had happened, or would it reset when they all woke up in the morning?

"Gilm," Corinne said.

Wait, did it work or not?

Geoff searched Corinne's face for answers, and she returned his gaze with the somber look of someone who was about to deliver terrible news. Just like the time Mr. Dent shared with the class that his favorite coffee shop was shutting down after its baristas attempted to unionize. That man did not like people organizing against authority.

Stage Fright and
the Looming Performance

"I'm just kidding," she said. "I'm fine. Rubber baby buggy bumpers. See?"

Geoff's dad raised his bushy eyebrows. "Wow, you said that really fast. I'm impressed. That's a tough tongue twister."

"Theater kid," both Corinne and Geoff said at the same time.

"Jinx!" they said at the same time again.

"You owe me a Coke," Corinne said.

"Maybe, but you probably won't even remember this," Geoff replied.

The room fell silent.

"What?" Corinne asked.

"OK," Geoff's dad said. "I'm going to go brew us a tea that helps with the comedown from some of the more intense spells."

Or something like that. Geoff was only half paying attention after the second-most traumatic experience in his life. It's not every day that you have a wish granted; have it turn against you and the world; go on a date with the girl of your dreams, knowing you'll lose her whenever the spell wears off; and then say something really stupid to ruin a moment.

And now he was going to have to have tea with her and his dad. Great.

* * *

Corinne wrapped both hands around her teacup while resting her elbows on the table. Geoff's dad sat blankly with one finger hooked through the loop of his cup. Each seemed to be replaying the day's events in their own way.

The flowery teapot set in the middle of the table was mesmerizing. At first glance, it seemed like any other ceramic teapot, but the more Geoff looked at it, the more he realized it was something else. What he'd initially mistaken as red roses were the open mouths of Venus flytraps. Or at least something like them.

Vines, which Venus flytraps definitely were not, twisted around the pot and its handle. Some were a deep green, like a mossy forest floor, while others were black as the feathers of a crow. Instead of a white background color, it was dismal grey, like a midwinter Portland sky.

Most of the teapots Geoff had seen had whimsical designs or soothing colors with a classic floral motif. But not this one. In fact, he slowly noticed a scene playing out across the vessel. He turned it a few times and looked for a pattern. What was the story telling him? Was that a bird? Was that a human face?

Just when he thought he'd figured out the pattern, it changed on the next rotation. The unglazed base of the pot grated against the tabletop.

"Can you not?" Corinne asked. "That sound is . . . unsettling."

"Sorry," Geoff said.

Geoff caught his father in a knowing smile. It was as though he'd wondered if Geoff would be curious about the teapot, and he was proud that Geoff saw a design unfold. Geoff couldn't know for sure, and he certainly wasn't going to ask in front of Corinne.

"Sorry," Corinne replied. "That came out a little harsher than I meant it to be." She turned toward Geoff's dad. "So, I'm not going to remember any of this tomorrow?"

Sure, Geoff was the one to have caught the fine print of the un-wish in the old book, but once he'd pointed it out to his dad, the professor had taken over and explained just why that was. Not only practically for the purpose of the spell, but in great detail on the origins of the compromise going back to . . . blah blah blah; Geoff ended up zoning out after a while.

"No," Geoff's dad replied. "Probably not."

"So, what will we all think of when we think of today?"

"What were you doing on this day three weeks ago?"

"I don't know," Corinne said. "Went to school, went home, worked a little bit at my dad's restaurant, did some homework, and went to sleep."

"And how often do you think about that day?"

"I haven't. Not until you mentioned it just now."

"Something like that."

"So, could I remember it when you mention it?"

"No," Geoff's dad said. "But no one else will remember either, so it won't come up. The only person in the world who will remember is sitting right next to you."

Corinne took a long sip of tea and then swirled the contents for a moment before turning toward Geoff. "I had fun tonight. Before, you know, the whole fighting my brother and finding out you almost cursed the whole world."

Geoff's dad stood up from the table with the old book grasped firmly in both hands. "I'm going to give you two some time. Nice to meet you, Corinne. I hope our paths cross again."

His dad nodded to Geoff and disappeared into his office.

Corinne stood with her empty hand held in the air, palm out. She stared back at Geoff with a quizzical, open-mouthed expression. She grinned and pumped her hand up and down as though she were shaking an invisible hand. "Nice to meet you too, sir."

Geoff chuckled under his breath. "So, you're not mad then?"

Corinne eased back into her chair. "Mad that you'd use your one wish to woo me instead of wishing for, like, ten million dollars? I'm flattered, honestly. Maybe if I had more time to think about it, I'd be mad, but since I don't, I'm not."

Geoff decided it would be kind of a mood killer to tell her that the book wouldn't let him wish for ten million dollars or that she was really lowballing how much money you should wish for, so he kept it to himself.

"Good," Geoff said.

"What are you going to do with all this extra knowledge you have over the rest of us?"

"I don't know. Rule the world, probably?"

"Oh really? Can we have some better spring holidays, then? It's a pretty drastic drop-off after Halloween, Thanksgiving, and Christmas."

"That's a great idea, I'll put that on my agenda." He acted like he was writing on invisible paper. "How about a festival to celebrate the rain? Like a little wooden gnome would fly from house to house on a bike pulled by river otters that would drop presents in people's wet socks hung over the fireplace to dry out."

"That sounds a lot like Christmas."

"I don't know what you're talking about. It's way easier for a little wooden gnome to fit down the chimney, plus it's like combining Santa and the elf that parents put around the house to shame their children into good behavior."

"So, by combining elements, you're making something new."

"That's right."

"Wouldn't a wooden gnome be afraid to climb down a chimney? Because of the whole wood-being-flammable thing."

"It's magic, Corinne. It's a wooden gnome that comes to life once a year. Besides, I think technically, Santa is flammable too."

She nodded like she was a judge and Geoff had just presented an airtight case. "The otters are a nice touch."

"It's all in the details, Corinne."

The two sat in silence for a moment. Corinne scanned the built-in cabinets for what Geoff's dad kept behind the glass. Like most shelves in the house, there was always more to see once you started to look closer.

She straightened up in her chair and cleared her throat. "No, really, what do you think it will be like having all this information that no one else has?"

You mean what's it going to be like tomorrow when you have no idea who I really am? When I'm back to just being the guy who sits next to you in Dent's class?

Geoff wanted to tell her everything. Literally explain every feeling he was experiencing right then, from the satisfaction of finally getting to know her to the fear of losing her in just a few hours. The soaring high he felt just sitting across from her that he'd have felt regardless of whether or not they'd just saved the world together.

Did it count as saving the world if you were the cause of the threat?

Didn't matter; they'd still done it. But why wouldn't he tell her everything he was feeling? She wouldn't remember it tomorrow. He could tell her anything.

Because that would be psychotic. It's our first date, and I don't want to ruin it even though I'm the only one who'll remember it. That's more of a third- or fourth-date conversation, probably.

Geoff had never been on more than two dates with the same person.

He took a sip of his tea.

At least he meant to take a sip of his tea. He'd drunk the last of it a few minutes ago, so now he was stuck pantomiming a tea-drinking motion and hoping she didn't notice. "I think the only things I really learned are that my dad may be some sort of dark wizard or something, and I like pizza that looks like a salad."

Corinne took a long sip of her tea. She swirled the contents of the cup and locked eyes with Geoff. Her cheeks were slightly flushed, and her lips a perfect cupid's bow.

"Well, I'm sure there is something useful in all of that. What about me? Did you learn anything about me?"

Here we go. Should I tell her everything I feel now? No, that's still for later, but I should tell her something real. She deserves to hear it, and I deserve to say it. Just don't blurt it out.

"I feel like I kind of confirmed more than I learned."

She cocked her head. "Oh? What's that?"

Look at her hands around that teacup. They could be in mine. We should at least hold hands. No, that would be weird. She's across the table.

Just do it, Geoff. This may be the only time you have to do this. Besides, if it's weird, she won't remember it.

Geoff stood and reached for her hands.

She stood from her chair and grasped his.

"You're as amazing as I thought you'd be," Geoff said. Her hands were warm and soft, and she curled her fingers into his.

"I'm jealous you're going to remember this, and I won't," she said.

"Remember what?" Geoff asked.

"Remember this," she said as she pulled him close for a kiss.

Breaking a String Theory

Geoff had developed a habit of checking the puddles in the broken sidewalk below to see if it was raining. Sometimes, the tiny rings formed by the drops were soothing to him, but there was no calming effect that morning.

He'd been replaying the events from the night before, over and over in his mind's eye. How the abnormally bright streetlight in front of their house made Corinne's grazel eyes sparkle. How her long hair shone despite being darker than the shadows of the night.

"You know, you should just kiss me tomorrow," she'd said. "So I can have a memory too."

"Just walk up and make out with you. Sounds plausible."

"What? It's normal. It happens all the time in musicals."

"One: I don't think that's true. And two: Dent would send me straight to jail. No detention, no principal's office, just straight to Multnomah County jail."

Corinne chuckled. "OK, so if you try something like that, just don't do it around Dent. You know, I've had a crush on you since the first day you walked into his class."

"Now you tell me," Geoff replied.

"What? A girl has to play it cool, Geoff."

He replayed how they held each other's hands on the sidewalk and didn't say anything for a long while.

"This isn't fair." She chewed on her lip. "There has to be a way to remember this. Any crush I've ever had fell apart after getting to know them. You're different. This is different. Even without the stupid song. Not that it's stupid." She stared at her intertwined fingers. "You know what I mean."

"I know what you mean," Geoff said softly.

She slid behind the wheel of the Subaru. "I'll see you tomorrow."

"Yeah, I'll see you tomorrow," Geoff said. He knew it wouldn't be the same, but he also didn't want to ruin the moment.

The door shut.

He stood in the street, his arm raised like a scarecrow for a long goodbye until her car's taillights disappeared below the crest of the hill.

As he stood in the attic of the old craftsman, he felt like he might as well be a ghost. No one at school would know him, just like the day before yesterday. Sure, Corinne might, but today he'd just be the jerk who made fun of musicals, one of her fondest pleasures. Or the arrogant kid who bragged about writing songs but couldn't meet her songwriting challenge. Neither a great look.

There was a bright side, however. At least Will wouldn't know Geoff had gone out with his sister.

A knock sounded from the door at the bottom of the staircase, and the hinges creaked as it opened.

"You're going to be late," his dad called. "Come on down. I made you some breakfast."

"Be right there," Geoff said. He took one last look out the window at the puddles below, grabbed his backpack, and padded downstairs.

Thunk!

What was that?

A protein bar bounced off the wall and fell to the ground as Geoff shut the door behind him with the heel of his shoe.

Geoff stared at his dad. The Smiths weren't athletic people. His dad couldn't throw, and Geoff couldn't catch.

"I thought you said you made me breakfast." Geoff leaned down to grab the protein bar off the floor. Luckily, it was still in its wrapper.

"I would have if my cast iron skillet wasn't left on the stovetop, filled with some sort of curious sludge."

"Oh yeah," Geoff said. "Sorry about that."

"What happened to your face?"

Geoff pinched the bridge of his nose. It had been sore and throbbing ever since he woke up, but he couldn't help but check in to see if it still hurt when he touched it. It did.

"Nothing."

"Well, I'm sure the other guy looks like a panda too. Maybe even a raccoon, huh? Which is better? Regular or trash panda? I don't know."

"Ha ha, Dad."

His dad's face softened. "Sorry, kid. Rough go, huh?"

"Yeah, kinda."

"You want to talk about it?"

"You wouldn't understand," Geoff said.

His dad nodded as he filled his thermos with coffee. "Try me."

"It's complicated." Geoff was almost thankful no one knew him at school. This type of conversation with people who couldn't remember anything from the day before would get annoying pretty quick.

His dad twisted the lid shut on his thermos, set it down, and leaned against the counter. "Like 'breaking the curse from a wish that got you a little notoriety and a date with a really nice girl, but now no one remembers, including the nice girl' kind of complicated? Or is it something else?"

"Wait." Geoff replayed everything his dad had just said, but slower, in his head. Then he played it again but with a funny high-pitched voice. Then one last time, in his dad's actual voice. *How could he know that if everyone forgot?*

"How can you remember that?"

His dad crossed his arms and toed the edge of one of the oversized hexagonal tiles of the kitchen floor. "I don't."

"I'm confused," Geoff said.

"The last thing I remember is waking up from a dream where Olep Hjalmar was dragging a brass pen

out of my office. Other than that, the day, the night—
everything is a blank."

"I'm more confused. Who is Olep Hjalmar, and
why would he be dragging a brass pen? Like you
would have to lean down to drag a pen, unless the pen
was huge—"

"You know Olep Hjalmar. He's watched over us
your entire life. Your grandfather brought our little
gnome friend back from a trip to Denmark. Also, it
was just a regular-sized pen."

*The gnome in his office? Interesting that Dad calls
that a dream. Any dream with that little wooden freak
in it is a nightmare as far as I'm concerned, and knowing that he has a name just makes it worse.*

"I didn't know you named him," Geoff said.

"I didn't." Geoff's dad grabbed the handle of the
skillet and brought it over to the trash can, where
he emptied its contents. "Anyway, I just noticed the
distinct smell coming from your little makeshift cauldron here, and it reminded me of a new acquisition.
A carved-leather-bound tome I explicitly asked you to
ignore."

"Not really. You just kind of held it tight and disappeared into your office."

"It was implied."

Geoff huffed out a laugh. "OK, maybe it was
implied."

"Anyway, it seems I wrote myself a lengthy note
last night detailing everything that went on here, so . . .
I'm sorry, son." His dad set the skillet back onto the

stove and crossed the room to give his son a hug. "But I'm proud of you."

Geoff gripped the back of his dad's shirt and hugged him as hard as he could, like when he was a little kid. "I finally found my place here. I had an identity. People not only accepted me, they were glad that I was here. I was glad to be here, but now it's all been ripped away like it never happened."

"I know, son, I know. I'm sorry."

"And I really liked her."

"I know, son. I know."

Geoff sniffed and let his father go. "I didn't know you could do that. You know, that you could just write it all down."

"I didn't either," his dad said. "I'm surprised it worked, to be honest. Magic does a pretty good job of wiping technology for some reason, but not always with pen and paper . . . or quill and parchment." His dad started to stare off. "Stone and chisel—"

"I get it," Geoff said. "At least someone knows. Hey, why didn't you share that information last night? You know, with Corinne?"

"I don't know, Geoff. I'm sorry, I don't remember."

"Oh yeah." Geoff stared at his shoes through watery eyes.

Geoff's dad squeezed his shoulder. "Hey, kid." The look on his dad's face was as gentle as someone scooping up a puppy from a box of its fluffy little littermates. "You're going to be late to school."

The Unsettling
Set List

Geoff's stomach felt like he'd swallowed a cannonball covered in a tart candy coating. It wasn't the protein bar that his dad had given him earlier. That was a tasty chocolate-coconut flavor profile that went down easily.

No, his gastro issues had more to do with the guy at the bike racks staring straight at him like a laser blaster set to humiliate.

"Hey! Look at new guy's face!" Will said to the area, as though he had friends. "You look like you're turning into a panda. Are you turning into a panda, new guy? Hey, everybody, the new guy is like a were-panda. Quick, someone get me some silver."

As he approached the bike rack, Geoff realized something had shifted in him. Maybe his encounter with Will last night had awoken a new confidence. He wasn't sure why, since he'd been punched in the face. Maybe it was because he'd already experienced the worst-case scenario.

Or maybe, now that he knew that Will had been such a jerk to everyone his entire life, he was able to notice that people pretty much steered clear of him.

For the first time in all of their encounters, Geoff took a moment to observe the world around him instead of just focusing on the one guy making fun of him and imagining how that must make him look to everyone else.

Will was on his own.

As it turned out, no one really paid any attention to Will. Which meant that Geoff no longer had to carry around the sting of shame from being bullied. In fact, in that moment, he didn't understand why there was shame associated with it at all. The shame should belong to the bully. The one with strength or status who was constantly punching down on those with neither.

Geoff clicked his lock into place and stared his tormentor in the face. He wasn't mad. He wasn't interested in egging him on. He'd just had enough.

And that was all it took. Will seemed to realize that his easy mark wasn't so easy any longer. He quickly scanned the area until someone else grabbed his attention.

"Hey, Brandon," Will said to some other kid, presumably named Brandon. "Did your mom buy those shoes at the mid-2000s cartoon department store?"

Wait, it's as easy as that? Just stare back? Geoff squinted. *I guess it wasn't easy. I had to pack a lot of living into the past couple of days to get here, but really? I just had to nonverbally let him know I'd had enough, and he left me alone for someone less challenging?*

I guess it helps that he has no idea that Corinne and I are together. Were together. God. Today is going to suck.

Geoff shook his head as he paced toward the school and wished Brandon the best of luck. He knew he could, and probably should, stick up for the kid, but he'd already saved the entire world the night before, and his face still hurt. Along with other things, like his heart.

Come on, Geoff. You can't just walk away.

He snapped his fingers as an idea sprang to mind. It was risky. He knew the first part would work. It was battle-tested. Literally. The second part, however . . .

Will circled Brandon like a shark that announced its approach with sarcasm instead of ominous cello sounds.

"Hey, Will!" Geoff yelled.

Will rounded toward the sound. "What?" he yelled back.

Hopefully Brandon understands the art of the low-key head nod. Geoff did his best to nonverbally communicate to the kid that he had a plan. "Tell your sister I think she's hot."

Brandon mouthed *Thank you* and snuck off toward one of the side entrances to the school.

Will's face gathered all available blood and turned the reddest shade of rage Geoff had ever seen. He gritted his teeth and sprinted toward Geoff, his hands like knives cutting the air in front of him.

Geoff took off toward the the main entrance to the school as fast as he could, laughing like a maniac. The first part of his plan had worked, and now he prayed the second would as well.

Prayed, specifically. Not wished. If he ever made another wish again in his entire life, he would make sure it was for two billion dollars.

"Slow down, Mr. Smith!" Mr. Dent called from out of nowhere. "No running!"

"Sorry, Mr. Dent," Geoff replied as he slowed to a casual gait. He couldn't help but grin. He was getting pretty good with his on-the-spot plans. Dent must have had secret passages through the building to be seemingly everywhere at that school. Seriously, the man was practically omniscient, and once again, he was there the moment Geoff stuck a toe out of line.

"See you in class, Mr. Smith."

Geoff didn't even have to look back. He knew Will wouldn't continue his pursuit under the supervision of a teacher. Especially Dent. Like every good predator, Will knew when to cut his losses.

* * *

Geoff found his spot in the river of students. The current was strong during that time of morning as people hurried to their first class. He gave himself over to the flow with a head full of numbing dread. The buzz of his minor victory had already subsided.

Soon he'd have to meet the grazel gaze of Corinne Shelby. In an everyday world, one in which people remembered everything from the night before, those eyes would convey recognition, anticipation, or, if Geoff allowed himself to be so bold, elation to see him walking into Mr. Dent's classroom.

Why did she have to tell me she had a crush on me?

Maybe it was to make him feel better, or maybe it was to make her feel better. Unburdening herself of the secret. But she'd also confirmed his huge mistake in acting like he was above musicals. Like he thought they were stupid, but he was smart because he wrote songs.

No, the Corinne he was about to encounter was the day-before-yesterday Corinne. A Corinne who would probably feel vindicated by the failure of a kid who, for some reason, had made fun of something that she loved. A community she'd poured time and effort into building. As far as she knew, he couldn't write a song that rhymed the word "film."

Which maybe he didn't on his own, but whatever, it happened.

The flow of the hallway slowed to a trickle as he made his final approach to Mr. Dent's classroom. Geoff stared down the increasingly empty corridor. Just him, a handful of stragglers, and a sign-up sheet for the school musical.

I mean, I did say if I got out of the principal's office that I'd sign up . . .

He stared at the poster.

I'd still be on a stage in front of people singing; maybe that would be cool. Maybe I'd feel more at home when I finally do start a band here. The more hours, the better, right?

He grabbed a marker that hung by a string beside the sign-up sheet and scribbled away all of his free time for the next couple of months.

Maybe I need a break from songwriting, anyway.

Geoff exhaled a long sigh like that of a thousand-year-old man and stepped back to stare at his name amongst a half-dozen or so others. He assumed there were more on the other sign-up sheets and wondered how many people would be in the theater room later that afternoon.

He wondered what free time he was really giving up. Time spent alone in his room?

It was a weird feeling. Instead of dreading rehearsals with a bunch of strangers, he felt something else. It was confusing. He definitely wanted to get back in Corinne's good graces, but he realized that for the first time since he'd moved to Portland, he would belong to a group. He was going to be a theater kid, and he was looking forward to it.

"Sorry!" a kid said as he brushed Geoff's shoulder. Several other students rushed by to get through their classroom doors.

It was as though someone had turned off a spotlight that Geoff had willingly stepped into. He'd faded back from his imaginary center stage into the locker-lined halls of the drab old school.

Time to face the music, bud. First class, worst class.

He shrugged the straps of his backpack higher and strode toward the open doorway. He'd been dreading this moment all morning, but it had to happen eventually. He was finally going to see Corinne's face. Would it hold contempt? A side-eyed sarcastic smirk? Would she even acknowledge him at all?

The Power
of Song

Geoff didn't want to, but he had to look. It was instinctual to look where you were going, even if it was a few rows away, even if it put you in the eye line of someone you were afraid to see. His seat was empty, of course, but thankfully, so was the one next to it.

Corinne wasn't in class.

His shoulders relaxed, and he almost allowed himself a smile before the tightness crept back to take hold. He wouldn't have to face her today, sure, but he'd just delayed the inevitable. He'd still have to see her tomorrow or the next day.

Ripping off a Band-Aid hurts; everyone knows this. And everyone has their own technique. Some move slow, which is wrong. You have to just grab and go as fast as you can. For Geoff, the time between the decision and the action was just as bad as the aftereffect of plucking hundreds of tiny hairs away by the root all at once. And now he'd be stuck in anticipation of tearing away an industrial-strength Band-Aid until he saw her again.

Geoff trudged toward his desk.

No one whispered as he walked by. No one stared at him as he slumped into his seat and pulled out his spiral-bound notebook for notes. He'd reverted to a generic face in a game of classroom Guess Who.

He couldn't believe how quickly he'd acclimated to notoriety and wondered how long it would take for his mind to accept that he was back to being some kid that no one knew or cared to know. Maybe his mind would never reset.

He shrugged to himself. It was still better than listening to everyone talk using just one word or chant it together like a bunch of teenage zombies.

Teenage Zombie would be a pretty decent band name, though.

* * *

The routine of taking notes, packing up, and heading on to the next class was almost a comfort after the chaos of the night before. Outside of the occasional stare at his whole black-eye situation, he floated through a sea of faces without the slightest spark of recognition. The rows of lockers along the walls all looked the same, hall after hall, with the exception of sign-up sheets for the musical, posters for a school dance, and a couple of reminders to take social media breaks.

He stopped in the courtyard to stare at a poster in between classes. The first meeting for Wicked was that afternoon.

At least that would break up the monotony of the day.

Geoff wondered what the theater kids were like when they got together. Would they be cliquish or welcoming? Would they constantly do bits where they'd talk in accents and sing to each other?

He was pretty sure they would do the bits, but that was OK. He used to do stuff like that with his friends back home in Houston, and he missed it. He missed them.

He missed someone recognizing him, their face breaking into a smile. The way they hurried toward him to share some gossip, rehash a bit, or try out a new one.

He shrugged his backpack higher on his shoulder and marched toward his next class.

* * *

Everyone seemed to find their second wind after the final bell. Which they needed for their trip home, or to hang out with friends, or to go to basketball practice, or whatever.

In Geoff's case, it was the meeting for the musical.

He noticed that he was grinning for the first time all day as he entered the flow of students in the hallway. He was walking faster than he normally did, and with purpose. His shoulders were still tight, but the tension he'd been carrying in his chest loosened. His baseline anxiety had been replaced by the nerves of meeting new people, which was real and something to be nervous about. Geoff wanted to make a good first impression.

He glanced out the main doors to see Will holding court by the bike racks antagonizing kids like a lousy salesman on a car lot. Like, really bad. Like "Take this car, or take this fist" bad.

The *Wicked* meeting was already paying off. At least he wouldn't have to face Will again today. Geoff may have found a new self-confidence when it came to his bully, but he also still had two black eyes from one punch. That guy could really throw a right hook.

Geoff slowed his pace as he rounded the corner toward the auditorium. *This is it. Last chance to back out. No one knows you, and no one would notice that you didn't actually show up. Who knows if they even check the sign-up sheets? Wait. What if they don't want me? Can you get cut from a musical?*

He breathed deeply, shrugged his backpack higher, and marched around the next corner toward the theater room.

The doors were taller than the doors for all the other classrooms, probably to accommodate oversized set pieces or something like that. Whatever the case, they were wide open, and the chatter spilled into the hallway. It had a baseline buzz with emphatic outbursts.

He was right. They were doing bits with accents. And singing.

Too late to turn back now, Geoff thought as he crossed the threshold.

Tables were pushed back against the black-painted walls of the wide open room. Students sat cross-legged on the floor or on top of the tables, legs dangling; some whooshed around the space in various games of chase.

Two girls were fencing using cardboard swords.

"They're from *Peter Pan,*" a voice from behind him said.

Geoff knew that voice.

It was like in his nightmare where he woke up to that weird gnome staring at him. The weird gnome with a name. He froze for a moment as what felt like tiny ice crystals formed in his bloodstream.

The Big Finish

Corinne stood before him, or at least she did now that he'd turned around. She didn't look sick. She just looked like Corinne. But Geoff knew this wasn't the Corinne from last night, the one from the best date of his life—the one who was into the song he'd written based on her impossible dare.

It was essentially the Corinne from the day before yesterday who'd challenged Geoff to write a song that, to her, he'd never delivered.

But there was no contempt on her face, no sprung-trap smirk. Just her usual pleasant demeanor, with plenty of eye contact.

"What?" Geoff asked.

"The swords are from *Peter Pan,* not the girls. I think Becca is from Seattle originally."

"Oh, right," Geoff said. "Hey."

"Hey," Corinne said back. "I thought you said musicals were dumb."

Geoff shrugged his backpack higher up on his shoulder. It was time to face his mistake. He'd been overthinking it now for days. There she was. There he was. It was time to make amends. He cleared his throat and looked her straight in the eye.

"I don't know what you're talking about," he said.

"I've always loved musicals."

"OK." She stared at him with a blank expression. Like she was expecting something. Probably an apology.

Geoff pinched the bridge of his nose, which was a mistake. It hurt. He wasn't used to being punched in the face, so he was just learning the whole after-care routine. But that wasn't important just then; Corinne was. He shook his head. "Yeah, I was kind of a jerk when I said that. I didn't mean to be, but I was. I am really sorry."

"Well, that's unexpected. A guy who apologizes and then tries something new."

Hey, I am a guy who tries new things. First pizza salad, and now this. Look at me. "I guess I've been doing a lot of new things lately. Anyway, forgive me?"

Corinne gave him a lopsided smile. "Sure, it's not that big of a deal. I was just messing with you. I think it's cool you're giving this a shot. I'm glad you're here."

Geoff wanted to embrace the warm feeling coming from his chest, but the tension in his shoulders beat the chest feeling to his brain. *No big deal? No big deal. After all this? She was just giving me a hard time, and I've been overthinking everything?*

Yeah, that sounds about right, Geoff. Good lord, you really are your worst enemy.

Geoff stared at the ground for a moment. "Hey, where were you this morning? For Mr. Dent's class?"

"Oh, I, um—I was doing some reading." Her eyelids did the cute half-moon thing as she moved closer.

Her thumb grazed his nose as her fingers gently surveyed his cheekbone. "Who panda'd your face?"

"Is 'panda'd' a thing people say now? It's been happening all day."

"Yeah, when you have two black eyes and look like a human-panda hybrid, people will say it. Did you get in a fight?"

"I don't know if I'd call it a fight. More of an experience in getting punched," Geoff said.

A kid nearby shouted in a posh English accent, *"An Experience in Getting Punched,"* then sang, "Only at OMSI!" "OMSI" stood for "Oregon Museum of Science and Industry." It had an IMAX theater, which wasn't really important but was good to know if you ever wanted to watch a movie on an absurdly large screen in real-world resolution.

The kid leaped dramatically from a table and joined a group of friends on the other side of the room.

"Who did it?" Corinne asked. There was no glint in her eye, no wry smile. Her head slightly cocked as she stared at the various hues of purple and green around Geoff's eyes.

"It's no big deal—"

"Was it Will?"

"It's not important."

"It was, wasn't it? Will did that to you."

Geoff's eyes narrowed.

Corinne began to pace. Geoff had never seen someone do that in real life, just in movies to show anxiety or convey a detective working something out for the big aha reveal. "It's true," she said. "I can't believe it's true."

"It's true"? Why did she say "it's true"? That's a weird way to process that your brother is a bully.

Corinne stepped closer and spoke in a voice just above a whisper. "So, I read something this morning and couldn't believe it."

"You don't have to talk so quietly, it's super loud in here," Geoff said.

"That kid literally just yell-repeated what you said about getting punched, Geoff."

"Alright, good point."

"I read this little note that I wrote to myself last night. Actually, it was a really long, detailed note about a date that you and I went on. All this stuff happened, like my brother beat you up, you wrote a song that almost cursed the entire world, and then you kind of saved the world. Oh, and I introduced you to my favorite pizza."

Geoff couldn't believe what he was hearing. The heaviness that sat in the pit of his stomach dissolved away like cotton candy in water. "I like that you mentioned the pizza."

"It's good, right?"

"Yeah. It's great." Geoff stared up at the dark painted rafters and wondered aloud, "How is it that both you and my dad knew to write all that down?"

"I don't know," Corinne said. "I don't remember anything from yesterday."

Geoff nodded. "My dad said the same thing—"

"Except a weird nightmare about a little wooden gnome with a big brass fountain pen."

Geoff blinked. "Olep Hjalmar." The fact that the gnome had a name still kind of skeeved him out, but maybe the little creep wasn't a creep at all. If he hadn't been in the middle of one of the most important conversations of his life with the girl of his dreams, Geoff would have taken time to investigate his feelings on the fact that his worst nightmare had been turned on its head.

Corinne's eyes narrowed. "Bless you?"

"Nothing," Geoff said.

"You should just kiss me tomorrow," she said.

I mean, she said it, but that was in the moment. A different moment. Did she even write that part down? What if she didn't? Even if she did, reading it isn't the same as remembering it. Is it? What if I just remind her? Would that be weird?

Geoff's hands began to sweat, and his heart started to beat faster, like a song coming to its big finish in double-time snare beats.

Just say it.

"We kissed last night."

That was dumb. That sounded dumb, Geoff. I hope she wrote that down. Otherwise—

Corinne bit her lower lip momentarily as her eyes met Geoff's. "Yeah, I read that. I wish I remembered."

"Normally, I'd say you should wish for something great," Geoff said. "Like two billion dollars. But I think yours is better."

Geoff met Corinne's grazel gaze, and it was electric. The connection felt like they were picking up where they'd left off last night.

She wasn't looking away. A dimple creased her cheek. "You know, there's a scene in the play I'd like to rehearse."

"I, uh, I don't have a script or anything," Geoff said. "I didn't know I needed to bring one."

"It's OK, I know this scene. Just follow my lead," Corinne said as she leaned forward. Her hands landed gently on Geoff's chest.

His heart felt like it was bouncing against the inside of his sternum as he leaned toward Corinne.

Dude, what are you doing? This is crazy. Are we doing this in front of everyone? Yeah, I guess we are.

Their lips touched as his eyes closed, and the floor seemed to lift. It didn't, of course, but he had to take a moment to be sure. Once magic is introduced into your life, you start to question everything.

The room exploded with "oooooooh"s and "whoa!"s. Geoff pulled back and opened his eyes to meet Corinne's. She slowly blinked and pushed a strand of hair behind her ear.

"That was nice," she said. "A little weird since I don't remember yesterday and only read about it in an alleged letter to myself, but I've had a crush on you for a while, so—still nice."

Yeah, I know about the crush. Wait, does she know that I know? What if she doesn't? I wonder what she wrote down in her notebook. Maybe it would have been better if I waited—

"I said it was nice, Geoff," Corinne repeated.

Geoff obviously didn't mask anxiety well. "Just as nice as last night," he said.

"Yeah?" Corinne replied.

Geoff rocked back and forth on his heels. "You know, the audience adds a new element, though. I hope this doesn't awaken some sort of exhibitionism in me."

Corinne laughed and leaned into Geoff's chest. "You are an idiot."

"Hey!" a voice boomed.

The weight was back in Geoff's stomach, the one like a candy-coated cannonball. Was Will going to pop up everywhere? How did he keep finding him?

"There's no kissing scene in *Wicked,*" the voice said.

Geoff was confused. How would Will know about musicals? He tried to locate the source of the voice and fell upon the most likely source. A tiny man neatly dressed in pleated slacks and a cozy cardigan. His glasses rested just above his forehead.

Definitely not Will. Must be the theater director, Mr. Andrews? Nice first impression, Geoff.

"Sure there is," responded a voice in the crowd.

"Yeah, there's a kissing scene with Elphaba and Fiyero," said another.

"And Glinda and Fiyero."

"And Elphaba and Glinda."

The theater director pulled his cardigan together. "OK, well, y'all win this round, but no PDA, everyone. You're still in school."

"We're not doing the kissing scenes?" asked one of the kids from the tables.

Mr. Andrews brought his glasses down in front of his eyes. "OK, yes, we're doing the kissing scenes, but you know what I mean. You're really pushing my buttons, Miranda."

Corinne twirled to meet the director like a ballerina, or maybe just a theater kid who wanted to get their teacher's attention. "We were just running our lines, Mr. Yesandrews."

Geoff blinked with astonishment at how she was able to pull off that move at a moment's notice. He closed the distance to whisper in her ear. "I thought his name was Mr. Andrews."

She whispered back, "Yeah, it is. But there's this whole thing in improv to say 'yes and,' and so we started calling him Mr. Yesandrews instead of Mr. Andrews; it's this whole thing."

Mr. Yesandrews struggled to keep a straight face. He brought his glasses down to the bridge of his nose and eyed Corinne. "Well, I guess we have our Elphaba and Fiyero."

"What? That's not fair!" said the kid who'd yelled about OMSI earlier.

"Relax. I'm just being theatrical, Keith!" Mr. Yesandrews said with a dramatic wave of his hand. "Now, let's call this meeting to order!"

Corinne grabbed Geoff's hands and pulled them around her as she leaned back into him. Geoff's heart felt warm. He was happy. For the first time in a long time, he was truly happy. He couldn't believe his luck. He let his mind wander to what would come after the meeting.

Maybe they'd go get her favorite pizza again. Maybe they'd make out afterward. Maybe they would go on to live a long life together, have kids, maybe a dog—

"I said no PDA, Corinne and Mr. Panda guy!" Mr. Yesandrews exclaimed.

He'd find out soon enough. For now, it was just nice to have found a place where he belonged.

Acknowledgments

I want to thank some folks for their help in bringing this book to life. First off, thanks to Molly Tentarelli, without whom I'd never have realized what an earworm the song was. Thanks to Russ Chapman, without him, we wouldn't have a song or a story. Thanks for living halfway across the country! Thanks to Paul Constantine for his timing on the drums and encouragement in the group chat.

Thanks to Julie Scheina for editing! I appreciate your guidance and encouragement. Also, thanks to Aja Pollock for your copy edits! She didn't edit the acknowledgments, so I'm terrified I'm doing something wrong.

Thanks to Ellen Lampl for designing the cover. Your work is so good! Thanks to Jessica Reed for formatting the very words you're reading. If you're into the style, you have her to thank, and so do I!

And to you. Thanks for reading all the way through to the acknowledgments. You must have really liked it, huh? If so, please leave a review wherever you like to read reviews. If not, I'm sorry, no refunds. If you're interested in hearing the song that inspired the book, search for The Mars McClanes wherever you listen to music. It's the song titled GILM!.

About the Author

Brian Corley is the praised YA author of *Space Throne* and *Ghost Bully* as well as *GILM!*. He is also a song-writer and musician in the well-received rock band, The Mars McClanes, who have been recording for twenty-one years.

Not all authors can say that their novel started out as a song lyric, but for Brian, that's exactly what happened. *GILM!*, his contemporary YA magical realism novel, was released in conjunction with a new song of the same name, a collaboration with his band. What began as a writing exercise trying to find a word that rhymes with film, ended as a circuitous creative journey that spawned an energetic rock song and the kernel of an idea to write a thrilling fantasy story about a new kid trying to impress a girl.

Brian believes a great story is a good mixture of emotion and craft, something you can tell someone poured their heart into. For him, there's nothing like someone telling you what a passage or a lyric means to them. He hopes his stories evoke an emotion in his YA readers that stays with them long after the book is closed.

A member of the SFWA (Science Fiction & Fantasy Writers Association), Brian has received high praise from *Publishers Weekly*, *Kirkus*, and *BookLife*, among others, for his novels. He lives in Portland, Oregon, with his amazing dog, Brisket.